Loners

by

Marian Exall

Loners

Cover Art by *Tina Lynn Stout*

The Wild Rose Press, Inc.
PO Box 708
Adams Basin, NY 14410-0708
Visit us at www.thewildrosepress.com

Publishing History
First Edition, 2025
Trade Paperback Print ISBN 978-1-5092-6345-5
Digital ISBN 978-1-5092-6346-2

Published in the United States of America

Dedication

To Graham whose support for my writing has been unfailing, and whose copy editing skills are unmatched.

Chapter 1

John Williams, Medical Examiner, wore waterproof boots and a rubber apron that stretched from neck to knees. The apron was spattered with blood and other bodily fluids released during the autopsy. I had no protective clothing and stood well back against the wall. Although this wasn't my first time, I didn't relish a close-up of the human interior.

"So, John, what can you tell me? Cause of death? Time of death? Sexual activity? Defensive wounds?"

The M.E. turned towards me slowly to give me time to realize my mistake. "Detective Sergeant McQuarry,"—*uh-oh, I should have used his title*—"I will include my findings in the report. Right now, I could only speculate."

Well, go on: speculate. I encouraged him with a nod.

"Female in her thirties, average build, no obvious signs of disease or injury. No signs of a struggle, or recent sexual activity. Time of death—" he looked up at the wall clock, "between six and nine last night. Until I get the blood work and stomach content analysis back, cause of death is unknown. However, if you're asking me to guess—"

Oh, for Christ's sake.

"I'd say, possible drug overdose or poisoning."

He pulled the sheet up to the woman's neck and stripped off his latex gloves. The body had been found in

1

a doorway on a downtown commercial street. There was no wallet, phone or other form of identification. I was not looking forward to a long day of combing through missing persons reports.

I approached the mortuary table. "Any unusual scars, tattoos? Anything we could tell the public to help identify her?" The pale face already looked more like a wax model than a person. *Could have been me.* The thought flashed through my mind, dismissed at once. I knew better than to connect emotionally to victims.

"You're going to have to rely on DNA and dental records, I'm afraid." As Dr. Williams walked with me to the outer area, he shed his protective garb and some of his official manner. He was new in the job, a transplant from another state, and still feeling his way through the police department hierarchy. I wondered what he'd heard about me.

The dead woman's clothes were spread out on a counter: black wool pants, pale blue shirt, cardigan jacket with deep pockets—nothing in them, though, or in the pants. The underwear was good quality, lacy without being overtly sexy. The only jewelry was a pair of silver earrings and a watch, no rings. She could be a teacher or an office worker; she could be anyone.

"There's no point in sending the clothes for testing," John said. "I'll bag them up and have them over to your office today."

Back at the police department, I met with our press officer and explained that the Medical Examiner's office would be sending over a touched-up photo of the deceased's face. She could then craft a news release to be circulated to the media, asking anyone with information to come forward. Next, I collected files on all missing women in the right age and ethnic group. I'd start with the county, then enlarge the search if necessary, hoping a family member or friend would step up before I went cross-eyed with boredom.

At six, I closed the computer and went home. The squad room was already empty, my colleagues having drifted off to their usual watering hole over the previous hour. I hadn't been invited and hadn't expected to be.

The top-floor rental apartment with a distant view of the bay was fine, but I wanted to buy my own place. That wasn't going to happen. You needed family money to get even a starter home, and I didn't have a family. An only child, I'd lost my parents when I was sixteen. "Lost" being the acceptable euphemism for my father driving into a bridge abutment on the interstate with my mother in the passenger seat. It was raining; he was drunk. I emancipated myself, thanks to the insurance proceeds, and two years later moved to the Pacific Northwest to start a new life. The thing about starting a new life: wherever you go, there you are, the same smart-mouthed kid who pushed away anyone who wanted to get close. I had learned early to be suspicious, which made me a natural for law enforcement.

A flyer from one of those genealogy outfits lurked amongst the other junk mail in my lobby mailbox: "Find your roots!" They were barking up the wrong tree—familial or otherwise—with me. I threw the whole pile of mail in the recycling as soon as I entered the apartment.

After riding the stationary bike for half an hour, I showered and got into my jammies. Dinner needed to be a salad as I'd indulged in a burger and fries at lunchtime. By eight o'clock, I was stretched out on the sofa with my laptop. I found that film about octopi off the Cape of Good Hope and started streaming. Soothing.

By the next day, the media release had elicited no leads on the dead woman's identity, so I continued my trawl through the missing persons files. I had pinned the photo of the dead woman next to my screen for comparison as I pulled up each file. I found myself staring at the image. The thought that ambushed me yesterday returned: she looked like me—the same dark hair and high cheekbones, even the same too-large-for-beauty nose. My eyes were darker though; perhaps death had drained the color from hers.

About noon, I considered rattling John Williams' cage for the autopsy report, but decided that would be counter-productive. So far, I liked the guy. He could be thorny, but so could I. He was thorough, and I respected that. He'd probably chosen his particular field because he didn't have the social skills for family medicine. I could relate.

I was eating a sandwich at my desk when my phone rang.

"Detective Sergeant?" Talk of the devil.

"Oh, call me Christine, please," I jumped in.

"All right," he paused, then started again. "Christine, I just sent the report over on our mystery woman, but I wanted to walk you through a couple of things in it. As I thought, cause of death was a drug overdose: a mixture of tranquilizers and sedatives. Could have been accidental, but more likely suicide."

"Not a crime then," I responded. Identification of the body was now a lower priority.

"No, but still a mystery. I think I might be able to help solve it." He sounded pleased with himself. "The deceased had a rare blood disease—Paroxysmal Nocturnal Hemoglobinuria. It's an incurable disease with debilitating symptoms. You can live with it for years but it's not fun."

"Motive for suicide, then?"

"There's more. The disease is rare, and so is the woman's blood type: she's AB negative—less than one percent of the population have that blood type. Those two rare characteristics make it likely that she's on a medical register somewhere. I could dig around and see if I can find anything. It'd be easier for me to do than you."

"Wow, you'd do that? Thanks, I appreciate it, John."

"Well, it'll take some time. I have dead bodies to cut up, you know." He sounded gruff, as if embarrassed at being caught out in a generous gesture.

I entered the dead woman's details, including the autopsy findings, into the national missing persons database, and turned to other work. However, I wasn't ready to take down the woman's photograph. The likeness fascinated me.

****

About a week later, my phone rang as I entered the squad room.

"Hello, this is Dr. Edgar Luchinski. I'm calling from Philadelphia. Dr. Williams gave me your number. I believe the woman whose body was found in your jurisdiction is my patient, Victoria Hartman."

My eyes flew to the photograph. "Oh. Can you put me in touch with her family? I'll need someone to identify the body."

"Well, Victoria had no close family—no family at all, really."

"What about friends? Her employer?"

I heard the doctor sigh. "No one, as far as I know. Victoria lived here all her adult life. Alone."

I was bewildered. Why had this woman crossed the continent to kill herself on my patch? *A loner like me*, I thought, before rejecting the comparison. I was alive, she wasn't.

"I last saw Victoria a couple of months ago. She failed to keep subsequent appointments. I was concerned and called the local police to do a welfare check at her apartment. It was empty. They found out she'd terminated her lease and got rid of her furniture, car, everything. Her bank account was closed. As for employment, Victoria hadn't worked for more than a year because of her illness. She basically erased her life before she left."

I let the silence stretch while I processed this. I should be asking how to locate her dentist so that we could compare dental records, but I was curious to know something else. "Tell me about Victoria. What was she like?"

"I didn't begin treating her until she became ill, but I took a complete history. Victoria was adopted as a baby by a couple in their late forties. She only found out she was adopted after her father died recently—her mother had died earlier. She told me she was trying to locate her birth mother, but the adoption was thirty-five years ago, and records had been lost. She said she felt betrayed by her adoptive parents—that they'd kept the secret of her adoption from her." The doctor paused, then seemed to collect himself and went on in a more businesslike tone. "You asked what she was like. It's hard to separate Victoria from the disease. I'd say she was quiet, self-contained. One of the primary symptoms of PNH is extreme fatigue, so it's hard to say what she was like when she was healthy."

****

A few weeks passed. I immersed myself in other cases. I'd shared a couple of lunches with John Williams, so when the M. E.'s name appeared on my phone, I thought maybe he was going to escalate with an invitation to dinner. I wasn't displeased with the idea.

"Hi, Christine. I wanted to let you know that, as no one's claimed the body, I have to release Victoria Hartman for cremation—"

"No!" A pauper's burial is not a burial—it's a complete eradication, as if she'd never existed. I felt a connection to this woman; I couldn't let her go. "I'll take care of it. What funeral home has she been sent to? I'll call them."

John gave me the details and surprised me with a call a couple of days later to volunteer to come with me to pick up the urn. We planned to go out for a quiet meal afterwards, and then, under cover of darkness, scatter the ashes in the bay.

The restaurant was nice. Conversation flowed. As we finished the wine, my thoughts returned to Victoria. "I still don't understand why she came all the way from Philadelphia to kill herself here. Perhaps she did one of those ancestry searches. Perhaps…"

"…you're sisters," completed John.

I blushed. I had of course entertained that possibility. It was ridiculous. Was I so needy that I had to invent a relationship with a dead woman?

"Yes, I saw the resemblance immediately," John continued. "You know, we still have her DNA results in

7

the file. I never ran a comparison because we identified her through other means. We could—"

The waiter was hovering, trying to persuade us to have dessert. We declined and asked for the check. I reached for it, but John was quicker. "Let me. You can pay next time." That sounded promising.

As we walked to the car, he explained that he wouldn't have to run the DNA check against the whole database, only the local law enforcement segment. Like all police officers, my DNA was on file in case of any crime scene contamination.

"But are you allowed to do that? Wouldn't you get into trouble?" I asked.

He stopped walking and turned to face me. "I can see you need this," he said, his voice serious, but then he shrugged. "It'll take less than take five minutes to run the comparison, but if I don't do it, you'll spend the rest of your life wondering, what if Victoria Hartman's your long-lost sister?"

When we arrived at the Medical Examiner's office, it was in darkness. We left Victoria's ashes in the back seat and entered, using John's keys. It took a bit longer than five minutes to retrieve Victoria's file from archives and set up the segment search with local law enforcement. While John was doing this, I stood at his shoulder and thought about his perceptiveness. I'd spent a lot of energy on my tough-girl image over the years, only to have this guy easily nail my foolish delusion that I could conjure a family out of a corpse. I'd been surprised at his offer to run the test, but now I realized he was right: I needed it.

The words flashed on the screen: NO MATCH.

I felt a wash of sadness and the prick of tears before

I pulled my shoulders back and took a breath. What could I possibly want with a dead sister who left no history to connect to? No, I was just feeling sad for Victoria: she must have been so lonely.

John shut down the computer, stood up, and looked hard into my glistening eyes.

"We'll never know why Victoria came here to die—probably a random choice, but the science doesn't lie: she has nothing to do with you, and that is that." John made the statement with such a show of conviction, I couldn't help stiffening. What was his agenda? He didn't know me well enough to realize that his attempt to get me to move on from Victoria had the opposite effect.

Chapter 2

When John Williams moved to Coalport he was looking for a fresh start. He was *not* looking for another relationship. He'd lived with Nancy for five years in Tucson. They didn't marry—never even discussed it. Neither of them wanted children; formal marriage seemed unnecessary. They each had their own bank accounts, insurance, and cars, and shared expenses for the condo, which was in John's name. What they also shared was a commitment to their jobs and an ambition to move up. To their friends they may have seemed more like amiable roommates than lovers, but—to John at least—they were as well-matched in bed as they were in life. He never imagined Nancy wanted anything different.

The night before his panel interview for a tenure-track position at the University, Nancy announced she was moving to Washington D.C.

"Roberto Carminez has offered me a job." Carminez was the new Democratic congressman for their district. Nancy had worked hard for his campaign. John had supported him with dollars only—politics wasn't his thing.

"But you're a graphic designer, for God's sake. What are you going to do in Washington?"

"Manage his website and social media, press relations—I'm his new Communications Director. Plus,

I'm thinking of going to law school—Georgetown. I've applied to take the LSAT."

"Don't be silly. You're thirty-eight years old!" The moment the words were out of his mouth, he knew he'd made a mistake. Nancy's face colored and her mouth set in a hard line. But John was on a roll. "You're sleeping with him, aren't you?"

She gave him a pitying look, shook her head—not in denial, but in disbelief at his stock reaction—and silently left the room.

He didn't get the job. He blamed Nancy at first for his poor interview performance, but after the sting of rejection wore off, he admitted to himself that wasn't fair. He was a medical doctor, not a Ph.D. Yes, he'd taught a few courses to pre-med students, but his primary job was as a forensic pathologist at the university hospital. The research he had published on different kinds of blood analyses was deemed insufficiently "academic." In other words, it had practical use for law enforcement but not enough polysyllabic words.

If Nancy could make a radical lifestyle change, so could John. He applied for the medical examiner job in Coalport, Washington on a whim, sold his walking-distance-to-downtown condo in a week, and bought a hundred-year-old farmhouse on three acres. He planned to spend his spare time on DIY projects, perhaps take up hiking or mountain biking: solitary hobbies—no relationships.

Nevertheless, he was intrigued by Christine McQuarry. The new job brought him in frequent contact with the police department. She stood out from her peers not only because she was the only woman detective in the squad, but also because she was twice as smart as any of her colleagues in spite of an apparent lack of formal education. She had a hard-edged brilliance about her that challenged people and kept them at a distance. John could see she might have a difficult job making friends.

Detectives don't usually attend autopsies unless foul play is suspected. This was a borderline case: a well-dressed and well-groomed white woman found dead in a doorway, no injuries or other signs of violence, but still a suspicious death. As soon as John had a closer look at the body, he was certain it was a drug overdose—accident or suicide.

But the body bore an uncanny resemblance to Christine, so he invited her to the autopsy. He was interested in seeing Christine's reaction; perhaps she would reveal something that would give him a clue to her prickly personality. In retrospect, that was a mistake. He had not anticipated that she would identify so closely with the deceased that discovering her identity would become an obsession.

Because he felt responsible, John had offered to help clear up the question of the dead woman's name. That was easy enough, given the markers of her unusual blood type and rare blood disease. He knew of Edgar Luchinski through one of his research papers, and it was a lucky chance that he was Victoria Hartman's doctor.

Even though a DNA comparison ruled out that Victoria and Christine were long-lost siblings—a test that breached all kinds of protocols and put his job at risk—Christine was still pursuing inquiries.

And now she was putting her own job at risk: there was no justification for questioning his conclusion of probable suicide.

The case was closed.

Chapter 3

John and I were different. He was a scientist: he dissected, extracted, analyzed, and then moved on. I worked on intuition: I attacked a problem like a dog with a chew toy, worrying it, tossing it in the air, shaking and nipping at it until I had a handle on a solution. Even our similarities drove us apart: our mutual thorniness attracted, but kept us at arms' length, like sparring partners.

John disapproved of my plan to go to Philadelphia to investigate Victoria Hartman's life and death further.

"Why can't you let it be, Christine? What do you hope to achieve?"

"It's only three days. I'll lose the leave if I don't take it this year. And the flight was ridiculously cheap." I knew none of my rationalizations answered his questions. To be honest, I didn't know the answers—only that going to Philadelphia and digging into Victoria Hartman's history had become a fixation.

John exhaled and closed his eyes in frustration. I shook my head; he was so annoying—always playing the sensible adult. Before I said something that would escalate our exchange into a row, I told him I'd see him at the weekend when I got back, and left.

I took the red-eye to PHL and a cab to the large medical center in Lower Merion Township where Dr. Luchinski had his office. With two hours to kill until our appointment, I found a coffee shop and downed two espressos which, on top of missing a night's sleep, left me twitchy. Even though it was raining slightly, I tried to calm myself by walking around the neighborhood, taking in lungfuls of East Coast air. I had spent the first eighteen years of my life not far from here, over the state line in New Jersey, but it didn't feel like a homecoming. I hadn't kept in touch with school friends or any surviving relatives.

As nine o'clock approached I entered the complex, located the right suite number, then ducked into a restroom to repair the damage the rain had done. My face in the mirror looked haggard. I splashed myself with cold water, then rubbed some color into my cheeks with paper towels. Although I never wore makeup, I could have used some lipstick then—to bolster my confidence if nothing else.

A receptionist in scrubs led me back to Dr. Luchinski's office. He rose from behind a desk and approached with hand outstretched. He was a small man in his late sixties, head shaved to white stubble, sad brown eyes in a thin face.

"Thanks for seeing me. I just wanted to chase down some loose ends regarding Victoria Hartman," I said, trying for a relaxed smile.

The doctor looked at me with narrowed eyes, not buying it. "You've come a long way for loose ends. A phone call would have been easier."

"Well, I had the time. I'm from South Jersey, so…" I didn't want to lie, so I let my voice trail off. No way was I going to confess that Victoria Hartman had become a fixation. "Do you have her last address? And maybe the name of her last employer?" I could see a folder on the desk. I hoped it contained Victoria's records.

After a pause, he responded, but he didn't open the folder. "Probably. Is there some question about her death? Whether it was suicide? I understood the case was closed."

I wondered how much I'd have to give away to get the information in the folder. I leaned forward, meeting his eye with my sincerest gaze. "Yes, it's officially closed, but I'm still puzzled about why she came all the way to the Pacific Northwest to kill herself, and why she made such an effort to hide her identity."

He nodded and allowed himself a small smile. "So it's personal. I thought it might be. You look a lot like her."

"Yes, I know, but we're not related—no DNA match," I admitted with a sheepish shrug. Honesty was always the best policy. I'd brought my police badge and business cards with me, even though I was outside my jurisdiction. I was relieved I didn't have to pretend I was here in an official capacity with the doctor. "The parallels between her life and mine keep nagging at me: looks, age, no family, even coming from the same area of the country. My—" I'd almost said, my boyfriend, which would have been a gross exaggeration of the relationship—"colleague thinks it's just a random coincidence. He's probably right. What do you think?"

Dr. Luchinski gave the question some thought. "Well, I'd have to agree with your colleague, although I understand your frustration. And to some degree I feel frustrated too. I knew Victoria as well as anyone knew her, maybe better than *anyone* knew her these last few months. She confided her shock at finding out she was adopted, and then her disappointment when she couldn't find out anything about her birth mother. Beyond that, I didn't really know her. She managed to hide how depressed she was. I suppose I feel guilty: I'm a doctor, I should have understood her mental state—should have referred her for therapy, though I doubt she would have gone. She was a private person, seeking psychiatric help would have been hard for her." He stared out of the window at the gray November sky. Then, pulling himself together, he opened the folder. "Here, I'll write down her address for you. Maybe you'll find a neighbor with more knowledge." He thumbed through the contents of the file. "Her employer's name is here somewhere—they continued to cover her health insurance while she was on disability leave and called me for a report periodically. She was the office manager at a law firm, but she hadn't been at work for a while."

He wrote some details on a pad of paper, tore off the sheet and handed it to me. I checked that I could read the information—doctors' handwriting is notoriously bad—then rose to my feet. "Thank you, Doctor. I appreciate your help."

I left him gazing out of the window again. I think he cared for Victoria and felt he had failed her. If I found out anything material, I'd get back to him.

I made my way out of the building. The rain had stopped. I asked a hospital worker furtively smoking a cigarette a few yards from the entrance if she recognized the apartment address on the piece of paper I'd been given. She told me it was ten minutes' drive towards the center of Philly. I summoned an Uber, and while I waited, looked up Victoria's employer on my phone. Stein Pinter was a law firm with offices on the thirtieth floor of a building downtown. Established in 1980, its thirty lawyers pursued a general business practice including real estate, corporate law, litigation, etc. etc. The website reeked of respectability. I doubted my leather jacket and jeans would generate much respect, but my backpack only contained a change of underwear, socks, and T-shirt, so I'd have to rely on my personality to impress them. Fat chance.

But first, I was going to scope out Victoria's home life.

The apartment complex where she had lived comprised of three four-story buildings spaced out in a park-like setting. There was a swimming pool (covered over now), tennis courts and a club house. In spite of the wintry weather and leafless trees, I could see how Forest Park earned the caption "luxury apartments." Victoria's place was on the top floor—another parallel with my life, but not a significant one. I called the apartment from the entry phone outside, wondering if anyone would be home. The complex clearly catered to childless young professionals who would be at work in the late morning. A man's voice answered. I said my name and explained that I was an investigator making enquiries about a former tenant, Victoria Hartman.

"I don't think I can help. I never met her." An Indian accent, light and lilting.

"It will only take a few minutes of your time." A pause, then the entrance door buzzed open.

The man who opened the apartment door was of South Asian origin, in his twenties, dressed in sweats.

"Hi." He smiled and led me into a minimally furnished living room. Two computer monitors stood on a large table against the wall. "I work from home, and I only moved in a month ago, so I haven't had much time to settle in." He introduced himself as Arun Shah, explained he was a programmer, and I repeated that my questions wouldn't take long. Then I got down to business.

"Did you know that Victoria Hartman lived here before you?"

"Yeah, I got some mail addressed to her, and the lady who lives across the hall mentioned her name. Has something happened to her?"

"I'm afraid she died."

His face showed appropriate concern, then his eyes lit up. "Was she murdered?" I expect he was bored, working alone in a near-empty apartment. The idea of violent death added interest to his day. He hadn't known her personally so I could forgive his eagerness.

I forced a laugh. "No, no. Nothing like that, just some loose ends that need tying up."

"Oh, I see. You represent the estate." He looked disappointed.

"Mmm." I hurried on. "You said you had some mail for her?"

"Yeah, I suppose I should have handed it in to the management office, but I forgot about it. I'll get it for you."

While he disappeared down the corridor, I remained standing, internally debating the legality of taking her mail. I hadn't asked for it—he'd volunteered. If he handed it in to the management office they'd probably junk it. Shah returned with a grocery bag. I glanced in: mainly advertising; I'd go through it all later.

"You said your neighbor knew Ms. Hartman. What's her name?"

"Mrs. Bell. Nice lady. Chatty, you know. She'll be

at work right now."

I pulled out a business card, requested he give it to Mrs. Bell and ask her to call me. His eyes gleamed again.

"I certainly will, Detective Sergeant," he said. "And shall I contact you if I get more mail?" He seemed not to have noticed the name or location of the police department I worked for.

"Yes, please." I left him still staring at the card. Just in case, I knocked on the apartment door across the hall, but as predicted, no one was home.

The caffeine had worn off, and I needed to eat something before I braved the lawyers of Stein Pinter. I found a café in a nearby strip mall and sat down with a large chicken sandwich and a soda to go through Victoria's mail. I separated the obvious promotional mass mailings, some skillfully personalized and marked urgent, and was left with a couple of good quality envelopes with first class postage. One had the return address of the Ditton Foundation and the other came from an individual, J.C. Burton. Both were located in Philadelphia.

The Executive Director of the Ditton Foundation wrote in effusive terms to thank Victoria for her most generous donation. She added a handwritten personal note, emphasizing how many children's lives would be improved by Victoria's gift. My eyes bulged when, at the bottom of the page, I saw the tax receipt information: Victoria had given the Foundation $178,600.

J.C. Burton was the Board President of the Ditton Foundation. His card was handwritten, and again thanked Victoria for the donation, inviting her to attend an open house at the Oreola Children's Center on October 23. Victoria died on October 13.

The Ditton Foundation didn't appear to have a website. A google search turned up an entry in the Directory of Charities and Nonprofit Organizations. The Foundation made grants to fund youth projects in the Philadelphia area. There was an online form to apply.

I pondered the information. I thought the size of the sum donated might represent Victoria's total assets: the proceeds from the sale of her car and furniture, and any savings. Was the choice of the Ditton Foundation as random as her place of death? Or did both have a logic I was still to unravel?

In spite of the calorie refuel, I was fading fast, and I still had the law firm to visit.

Chapter 4

A text from John came in as I crossed the atrium of the steel-and-glass building where Stein Pinter occupied the top floor: *How's it going?* Was this meant as an apology or the segue into an "I told you so" exchange? Either way, I didn't want to deal with him. *Fine. Call u later*, I replied, then switched the phone to silent.

The elevator doors opened straight onto the firm's lobby. In contrast to the gleaming marble and soaring space of the atrium, the décor here was traditional: dark wood and leather couches that gave the feel of a private club. Everything about it screamed money and power, with a subtext of "you don't belong here." I crossed an acre of priceless Indian carpet to reach the reception desk. The receptionist was beautiful: porcelain skin, large eyes and honey-gold hair falling in sculpted waves to her shoulders.

"I'd like to speak to the office manager," I said, feigning assurance.

The receptionist stared back without expression. A little young for Botox, I thought, but what else could explain the immobility of her face?

"We don't have an office manager. Do you mean the firm administrator?"

I nodded. "Do you have an appointment?" she continued.

I ignored the question. "It's in regard to a former

employee, Victoria Hartman." I offered her my card, which she looked at for so long I thought she might be dyslexic. The eyebrows never moved and the brow remained unfurrowed.

"Please, take a seat."

I wandered off a few steps but remained close enough to monitor her side of the phone conversation, presumably with the firm administrator. She relayed the facts without inflection or elaboration, then turned to me. "Ms. Romano will be out shortly."

I did take a seat then, and glanced at the reading material arranged on the low table in front of the sofa: today's *Wall Street Journal* and *Philadelphia Inquirer*, an *Architectural Digest*, and a local lifestyle magazine. I picked up the last on the off chance that the photos of recent charity balls and polo games might reveal the powers behind the Ditton Foundation or the Oreola Children's Center. No luck.

After ten minutes, a plump woman in a tailored pants suit and a fashionable bob approached with a smile. "Good afternoon, Ms. McQuarry. I'm Ruth Romano, firm administrator." She gestured at the older man in a conservative suit who had followed her into the lobby. "This is Jerome Pinter, our managing partner. Shall we?"

Pinter nodded to me but did not offer his hand. He was a distinguished-looking gent in a thousand-dollar suit. The silver hair set off a tan that probably came from a midwinter Caribbean break or the slopes at Aspen. Ms. Romano led us into a conference room behind the reception desk. A wall of windows looked out over downtown. The lawyer took a seat at the head of the table and indicated I should sit at his left. Ms. Romano took a place farther down the room and eased her chair back.

Clearly, Mr. Pinter was in charge of this conversation. He was holding my business card by the edges between finger and thumb as if afraid of soiling his hand.

"What is your interest in Victoria Hartman, Detective McQuarry?"

I noted that, while Ruth Romano used "Ms," he addressed me as "Detective." This might be the civilian equivalent of "good cop, bad cop." I was supposed to be intimidated by the managing partner. Unfortunately for him, attempts at intimidation tend to draw out my stubborn streak.

"She died in my town in suspicious circumstances," I responded.

"Oh? We were told she committed suicide. Tragic but hardly suspicious."

"How long had Victoria worked here?" I plowed on, ignoring his comment.

Pinter paused, then placed my card carefully in front of him. Was he going to throw me out? If he was considering that option, he decided against it. "Eleven years, the last one on disability leave. She started out as a secretary and was promoted to firm administrator four years ago."

I guessed he had answered because he was curious to know what I knew. I knew nothing, but his change of tack indicated to me there *was* something to know.

"What kind of employee was she?"

"Victoria was an excellent employee. The administrator position is key to the smooth running of the firm. She earned everyone's respect and trust. We were so sorry to hear of her death."

"But not sorry enough to claim her body or arrange for a funeral?" I kept my tone friendly, but the words were meant to provoke.

His tan deepened a little—anger or embarrassment? Neither showed in his voice. "That wouldn't be appropriate. Her family—" He broke off, perhaps remembering Victoria didn't have a family. "Why *are* you here?"

Time to come clean. "Victoria took great pains to become untraceable before she died. It was by mere chance that we found out who she was. She sold her belongings, terminated her lease, closed her bank account, and traveled across the country to a place where she had no connections. She got rid of any form of identification. I want to know why."

While Pinter considered this, I asked another question. "What do you know about the Ditton Foundation?"

He looked startled. "Why do you ask?"

"Before she left Philadelphia, Victoria made a significant donation there. It's a children's charity, isn't it?"

"Yes, a family foundation. In fact, Nathaniel Ditton was a longtime client of the firm. We acted for him in setting it up. But he's been dead several years."

"So she could have learned of the foundation through her employment here?"

"Possibly…" Pinter's attention wandered to the window view over City Hall. He seemed lost in thought. I sensed a shuffling behind me, as Ruth Romano prepared to speak.

"Perhaps Ms. McQuarry could assist us with our problem…"

"Hmm, perhaps." Pinter silenced her with a frown, before continuing. "The firm has very generous employee benefits, including a 401k retirement plan with a five percent earnings match. The disability plan also has a life insurance benefit." I couldn't see where this was going, other than to redeem the law firm's reputation after my attack on its treatment of a deceased employee. "Throughout her employment, Victoria made the maximum 401k contributions. Together with the life insurance payout, there's a considerable sum accumulated for the named beneficiary."

I waited a moment before asking, "And who is that?"

When Pinter didn't answer, Ruth spoke up. "That's the problem. We've been unable to find the person named as beneficiary for both the retirement account and the life insurance proceeds. Our Trust and Estates department has expertise in locating heirs, but they've come up empty. The next step is to place a legal notice in the newspapers of record."

"And the beneficiary's name?" I turned to face Ruth Romano, who seemed now to have Pinter's permission to take over the interview.

"Gaston Lemesur."

"Sounds French," I said.

She shrugged. "We don't know that Victoria had any connection with France. It's a real puzzle."

Pinter stood up, indicating the meeting was over. He shook my hand, muttered, "Good luck in your investigation," and left Ruth to escort me out.

"Were you friends with Victoria?" I asked as we waited for the elevator.

"Yes, well, I hope she regarded me as a friend. I was her assistant, we had lunch together most days but didn't socialize outside of work. I live in the suburbs and have a husband and little girl to look after. I liked Vicki, but she was a very private person."

It was the second time today I'd heard her described this way, but the first time anyone had shortened her name to Vicki. I wanted to prolong the conversation.

"So what were her hobbies? What did she do outside of work?"

"I'm not sure…she liked to read, I think. She ran— just for exercise, not competitively. That was before she got sick, of course. I wish I'd known her better, made more of an effort." She pulled a face. "I suppose we always says that, don't we? When it's too late."

I thought of another question. "When did she designate the 401k beneficiary? When she signed up for the plan?"

"No, she changed the beneficiary to Gaston Lemesur just a couple of months ago. She was on disability leave so she sent the form in. The previous named beneficiary was her father, and he'd died, so I didn't think too much about it at the time. You know, you look a bit like her."

I smiled, glad that the elevator had arrived and I didn't need to respond to her observation. I shook Ruth's hand and thanked her. She gave me her card and asked me to let her know if I found out anything. I said I would, then descended to the wide open spaces of the atrium again.

It was nearing five p.m. and rush hour was already in full gear. I'd booked a room in a mid-priced hotel near the airport—the downtown hotels were way too expensive—and I didn't fancy fighting through the commuter crowds. Besides, I needed a drink and a chance to process the information I had gathered. I found a pleasant-looking bar on a side street. It wasn't busy yet, so I snagged a booth and ordered a Negroni. I pulled out my notebook and jotted down what I had learned at Stein Pinter. I had several leads to follow: the foundation via the executive director or the board chair, possibly the children's center. There must be some significance to her large donation. And now the mysterious Gaston Lemesur. How thorough had Stein Pinter's efforts to find him been? Would it have been a priority for them? As I pondered my game plan for the following day, my phone rang. I didn't recognize the number, so I responded cautiously. "Hello?"

"Hi, Arun Shah gave me this number. This is Frances Bell, Victoria Hartman's old neighbor. I was so sorry to hear she'd died. I mean, I knew she was ill, but I didn't think she was *dying*. How can I help?"

This was the chatty neighbor. First impressions confirmed that description. She'd plowed into conversation without even verifying who I was. "Did you know Victoria well?"

"Oh, I'd say so. I moved into Forest Park about a year ago, after my divorce. I didn't have a job then, so Victoria and I had the place to ourselves during the day. You know she was on disability leave? Last summer, we hung out at the pool together most days. I'm working now though, which is why I missed you earlier."

"Did you know she was going to move out?"

"Of course! I bought some of her furniture."

"Did she tell you where she was moving to?" I was loving this: a source who appeared to have information and was eager to share.

"She hadn't made up her mind. A fresh start, she said, somewhere warm. She was going to just take off

27

and see where she landed. She had the money her dad left her, and I guess she was just bored with Philly. She'd lived here all her life."

This was a completely different Victoria than the person her doctor and her employer had described. "But what about her health? Didn't she have to continue getting treatment here?"

"Yeah, I don't know about that. She did tell me what she had—some kind of blood disease with a long name—but I got the impression that as long as she took it easy and got plenty of rest, that she could live with it. That's why I was so shocked when Arun told me she'd died."

"Look, I'd love to meet you and talk further. How about lunch tomorrow? Where do you work?" I needed to assess Frances Bell face to face. Either Victoria had been spinning her a yarn—why would she do that?—or there was a whole other story here.

"I'm in retail. I don't start work until ten. How about we meet for coffee at nine? There's a little coffee place near the store." She rattled off details of the location which I scribbled down. "Have to go—I've got a spin class starting in twenty minutes."

I downed the rest of my drink and looked at the time. The worst of rush hour should be over by now. I thought about calling John back as I'd promised, but he was three hours behind me, so I could wait until I checked into the hotel. I'd worked out that I could get to the airport via rapid rail from the 30th Street station a few blocks away. I paid my tab and made my way out of the bar. Night had fallen while I was inside. The sudden chill—and possibly the alcohol on an empty stomach—disoriented me for a moment. I was unsure which way to turn to reach the main drag. A man approached, hands dug deep into the pockets of his puffy coat, much better protection than my leather bomber jacket. I was about to ask him which way to Market Street when something—someone—jumped me from behind, knocking me flat onto the sidewalk. I felt grit under my cheek and an arm across the back of my neck. I couldn't move. I couldn't breathe.

"Wallet?" The voice came from feet above my head—I guessed the man I'd seen approaching. My assailant fumbled into the back pocket of my jeans and pulled out the leather folder containing my police badge.

"Fuck! A cop!" Running footsteps, retreating. A fist slammed into my temple. In best *film noir* tradition, a black pool opened in front of me and I dove into it.

Chapter 5

A patron who was leaving the bar saw my attackers running off. He helped me up and, with a hand under my arm, led me back inside. I'd been out less than a minute.

"What's this town coming to? A mugging downtown at six o'clock in the evening?" he grumbled as he sat me down at an empty booth. A couple of other customers crowded around. "We should call the police."

I started to protest that I was fine—a pretty obvious lie—when a man pushed through to offer me my badge and the backpack I'd lost hold of during the encounter. "She *is* police."

An older woman with heavy makeup leaned in to examine my face. "An ambulance, then. You might have a concussion."

I lifted a hand to my head. There was a tender spot but no blood. My palms were grazed where I'd fallen forward onto them. "No, I'm okay," I insisted, pulling myself together.

The barkeep came over with a glass of water, and the others moved back. "You sure?"

"Yes," I said with more conviction than I felt. I had the troubling thought that the attack was not a random mugging—that I had been targeted. The word "random" was woven through the story of the last few weeks: Victoria's place of death, her donation to the foundation, the recent change of beneficiary. Now the word seemed like a red arrow pointing to a pattern I could not yet see. I needed space and time to examine the thought. "I'm headed to the airport. How do I get to the 30th Street station?"

"No way you're walking five blocks on your own," the bartender said, taking charge. "I'll call you a cab. Up to you whether you take it to the station, or all the way to the airport."

I sat sipping my water and wishing for something stronger until the taxi arrived. I took the cab all the way. If I *had* been targeted, there was no sense in giving my assailants another chance. By the time I entered the lobby of the airport hotel, the right side of my forehead sported a swelling. More robin's egg than chicken's egg, but it hurt. While I waited to check in, I purchased cheese and crackers, a bottle of orange juice, and ibuprofen from the small commissary in the lobby. Not the dinner I'd planned, but I couldn't face a restaurant meal. I just wanted to lie down.

After the ibuprofen did its work, I took a shower and munched through my cardboard and fake cheese supper, with an orange juice chaser. Luckily the hotel didn't offer minibars to its guests, or I would have been tempted to knock myself out with alcohol. I was planning my itinerary for the next day when the phone rang. John. Shit, I'd forgotten to call him back.

"Hi. I'm sorry I didn't call like I promised. It's been quite a day."

John didn't acknowledge my apology. "How are you?"

"Great," I lied, eager to get to what I'd found out about Victoria Hartman. I took him through getting her old apartment address and employer's name from the doctor, the donation to the foundation, my visit to the law firm, and the mystery beneficiary named on her retirement account. I'd been rambling on for ten minutes before I realized John had said nothing, vocalized no reaction, not even a wow or sudden intake of breath. "Hey, listen to me running my mouth! How was *your* day?"

John didn't reply for a moment, then, "Christine, I'm worried." He sounded serious, like he was my high school principal or something.

"What? About me?" I laughed, feeling self-conscious. "You don't have to worry, I can take care of myself." I decided I would *not* tell him about the mugging. I wasn't going to encourage this proprietorial attitude.

"Yes, about you." John said. I wasn't sure how to respond. I wished we were in the same room so I could read his face and decipher his agenda. "Dr. Luchinski called me," he said after an uncomfortable silence.

That surprised me. "You're kidding! Why on earth did he call you?"

"He's concerned. He thinks you may be...overthinking Victoria Hartman's death. Obsessing even. He doesn't think it's healthy. Neither do I."

A sudden spurt of anger pushed me to my feet. *Obsessing, overthinking—I'm a detective, goddammit! It's what I do, it's who I am!* With an effort of will, I kept my voice light. "Oh, so you're a psychiatrist now, not a pathologist? And I thought Dr. Luchinski's specialty was diseases of the blood. I'm not his patient—where does he get off diagnosing me on the basis of a twenty-minute conversation? I went to him for information, that's all." My voice was rising; I dialed it back. "And I haven't even told you the best part. I had a call from Victoria's friend and neighbor. She sheds a very different light on the sequence of events." I explained everything Frances Bell had told me about Victoria moving away to somewhere warm, funded by an inheritance from her father. Again, John listened without comment.

When I finished, he said, "And you think this woman—whom you haven't met, by the way—is a reliable source?"

"I'm meeting her for coffee tomorrow morning. I'll assess her reliability then," I replied stiffly.

John sighed. "Look, follow up the leads you have tomorrow, but don't go chasing down rabbit holes. Get it out of your system and come back on Friday knowing you did what you could. When does your flight get in?"

"At one, I think," I replied.

"I'll meet you at the airport at one p.m. We'll go out for a late lunch. The weather's supposed to be great."

"Okay, if you want." This would save me waiting for the bus.

After we disconnected, I sat on the edge of the bed, staring at nothing. The hotel room was too hot, and my head hurt. I felt deflated, exhausted, drained of self-confidence. I should go over my notes again in preparation for tomorrow, but I lacked the energy. Having adjusted the thermostat, I climbed into bed and fell asleep.

I awoke what felt like five minutes later to a blast of cold air on my face. The room was now freezing. The luminescent numbers on the bedside alarm clock announced 1:43. I got up, peed, re-adjusted the thermostat, and got back under the covers. Sleep now eluded me. I tried deep breathing, counting with each inhale and exhale, imagining waves slowly breaking on the shore. After less than five breaths, my mind was jangling again.

What *did* I have, really? A sick woman tidies up her affairs, giving away her money to a good cause she'd heard about at work. The new beneficiary would turn up eventually: some lame duck she'd met and felt sorry for after her father died. She deflects the nosy neighbor with some tale of a new start, and then methodically sets out to find a faraway place with which she has no connection and where she can die anonymously. Eccentric? Perhaps. But maybe Victoria, through choosing the exact manner of her death, was asserting control after a life lived with little power or influence, where she felt she had been deceived by her parents and under-appreciated by her employer.

I remembered Ruth Romano regretting that she hadn't been a better friend to Victoria. "We always say that when it's too late," she'd said. Maybe, having unconsciously identified with a woman my age who looked like me, my efforts to find meaning in her death—to rehabilitate her in some way—echoed Ruth's wish that she had tried harder. My insistence in coming to Philadelphia perhaps said more about me than it did about Victoria Hartman.

So *was* I crazy? Fixated with finding a pattern where none existed? Were the doctor and John right—was my obsession with Victoria unhealthy, an attempt to fill some void in myself?

"Unable to sustain relationships"—this diagnosis (with a side serving of "anger management issues") had hung around my neck since my teens. I'd been in counseling even before my parents died, referred after I slugged another student, a Mean Girl who'd made some snarky comment about my clothes. I didn't take well to therapy, turning aside my counselor's earnest questions with flippant one-liners. The nature of counseling changed after my parents were killed. A new therapist tried to walk me through Kübler-Ross's five stages of grief, but I never progressed beyond anger and was glad to escape the whole process when I moved to the West Coast. In law enforcement, I'd had further brushes with psychologists—mandatory sessions after an officer-involved shooting or a particularly gruesome crime—and I'd become adept at demonstrating the appropriate thoughtful responses, masking my frustration with the psychobabble about "sharing feelings" and "opening up."

Alone and sleepless in a bland hotel room far from home, my façade of self-sufficiency crumbled. I felt exposed, vulnerable. Who *was* I, if I wasn't the hard-boiled detective, independent and clear-eyed, striding through the mean streets, untouched by doubt?

Traffic noise outside was increasing. The first planes of the day took off. My thoughts were repeating themselves in self-defeating spirals. I *had* to get some sleep.

****

I woke up feeling hungover, which was totally unfair given I'd only had one drink fourteen hours earlier. I put a complimentary coffee sachet and some water into the suspect machine next to the TV and, while it brewed, went to the bathroom to examine my face. The lump had gone down but a purplish bruise spread out from my hairline. I finger-combed my short hair forward to cover it. I didn't have time for another shower if I was to make my nine a.m. appointment with Frances Bell. I brushed my teeth and put on a clean T-shirt. Gulping down a cup of weak coffee and more ibuprofen, I checked the city transit map on my phone. Getting to the coffee shop Frances had named for our rendezvous would be complicated. My intention to economize went out the window; I summoned another Uber. Grabbing a donut on my way through the lobby—at least breakfast was free—I went out into the cold to wait for my ride.

The tide of self-confidence—which had ebbed so low in the night—had turned, replaced by a grim determination to do exactly what John had said: follow up on the leads I had developed, then leave the affair behind when I boarded the plane the next morning. There would be other cases to get my teeth into—cases with living victims to avenge. I wouldn't forget Victoria—she had left an indelible mark on my psyche—but as a cop I needed to retain a certain distance and objectivity. That's what I told myself.

Chapter 6

I arrived at my destination early and got myself another coffee—a decent one this time. I positioned myself, ready to make eye contact with any woman who scanned the room looking for a stranger. Frances Bell came in five minutes later. She was wearing a leopard print raincoat, tightly cinched, and shiny black boots with heels that looked dangerous. Her hair was blonde, too uniform in color to be natural. Eye contact made, she approached my table. After we'd introduced ourselves and she'd taken off the raincoat to reveal an expensive-looking black-on-black outfit, she equipped herself with an Americano—no cream, no sugar.

I got down to business. "What did Victoria tell you about her family background?"

Frances seemed eager to talk. "She lived in Philly all her life. Her parents are dead—her dad died just last year—and she has no brothers or sisters. Never married, although—" here she leaned forward with a conspiratorial gleam in her eye—"there had been a man in her life. I think he dumped her."

"She told you this?"

"Not in so many words, but there were hints, clues, you know. Like, I'd be telling her about my ex, what a lying scumbag he was, and she'd say how she'd been lied to as well, all men were bastards, that kind of thing."

"Hmm, she wasn't just sympathizing with you,

showing sisterhood?"

"Nope, definitely not. She was bitter. Then, another time, she said something like 'when I find him…' It was a threat. I think he ghosted her and she wanted revenge. She didn't give me any details—she wasn't that kind of person."

I waited for Frances to tell me that Victoria was a private kind of person—everyone else had—but she changed the subject. "She looked like you, same face shape, and that nice dark hair, but hers was longer."

I didn't want to go there so I asked another question. "How did she spend her days? She wasn't working, right?"

"She stayed home, mostly. She had appointments—you know, medical appointments. And she went to see the lawyer who was handling her dad's estate. That got complicated, apparently, and she had to go downtown a lot."

"The same law firm she worked for?"

"I don't think so. She said that firm only represented corporations and the super-rich. Another lawyer, I don't know the name."

"You said on the phone that she inherited money from her father. When did that come through?"

"Geez, must have been September, maybe beginning of October. I'd landed a job by then, so I didn't see so much of her."

"How much was the inheritance?"

"A *lot* of money! She didn't say exactly, but it was enough for her to relocate, get out of this city and see the world."

"She was going to travel?"

"I guess so. I would if I had the chance. The poor

thing had probably never been farther than New York. Anyway, she seemed really happy to be getting away, sold her car and furniture and everything. Shaking the dust of the city off her feet."

"Was she going to track down this man you think jilted her?"

"Oh, I hadn't thought of that. Maybe… Anyway, I didn't talk to her before she actually left. I'd started this job by then and joined a gym. You know, trying to get back in the swim of things. The divorce was devastating—took away my confidence for months. So I didn't get to say goodbye…" Frances voice trailed off, and she looked away, as if fighting tears.

"Did you know Victoria was adopted?"

Frances' eyebrows shot up. "No! She never said." She seemed affronted that her neighbor had not confided this fact. But then she nodded, narrowing her eyes knowingly. "That explains all the legal wrangling over the dad's money. She said something about competing claims. Perhaps the dad had an illegitimate child somewhere—his own blood kin—and he or she surfaced to demand a share."

This sounded like the plot of some cheesy TV soap, but I didn't comment.

"You're sure she got the money?"

"Absolutely!"

I asked more questions, trying to nail down specific things Victoria had said or done in the months leading up to her departure from Forest Park, but got mostly Frances' impressions and assumptions. After forty-five minutes, she glanced at her phone. "Gotta run or I'll be late for work. If I think of anything else, I'll call you, okay?"

After she left, I sat over the dregs of my cold latte and thought about what I had learned: a lot about Frances, and a few significant facts about Victoria. The inheritance was key. If it was, as Frances insisted, considerably larger than the donation to the Ditton Foundation, then the fresh start story might be true. Follow the money: the first rule of investigation. I had to find the lawyer that handled Victoria's father's probate to confirm the amount of her inheritance, and also to discover the facts behind the "competing claims" she had mentioned to Frances. What if Gaston Lemesur was Mr. Hartman's illegitimate son?

Shit, Christine! You're doing it again! Falling down rabbit holes, creating wild theories of the case when there was no case to pursue. Only a couple of hours ago I had made up my mind to finish my inquiries today and return home tomorrow for my own fresh start.

I drained my drink and refreshed the directions to the Ditton Foundation's office on my phone. Once I'd completed the next interview, I would relax, eat a nice lunch, and buy a book to take back to my hotel room. I had an early flight the next day.

****

The once-elegant brownstone that housed the Ditton Foundation's office as well as other random offices sat on a tree-lined street. The trees were bare now, and scraps of litter blew around their trunks. If I was following the money, not much of it seemed to have found its way to this neighborhood. Several of the shops were boarded up with "For Lease" signs. I climbed the steps to the front door and rang the doorbell. After a long wait, the door was opened by a Black kid about ten years old wearing a sparkling white polo shirt.

"Hello, is this the Ditton Foundation?" That's what it said on the tarnished plaque next to the door, but I hadn't expected to be greeted by a child. He nodded. "Is Andrea Faber here? I'd like to speak to her."

"She's on the phone." The boy turned and led me down a corridor to a large room at the back furnished with file cabinets along the walls and three desks, one of which was occupied by a fortyish white woman with wild hair. Her clothes were nondescript: business casual with an emphasis on casual. She waved at me to take a seat across from her and continued her phone conversation. I turned to thank my escort, but he had disappeared.

"Yes...I know...I know...I can't—look, I've got someone with me. We'll talk later....No, I'll call *you*." She disconnected and frowned at me. She was either still angry from her phone call or had taken an instant dislike to me. I smiled benignly back at her.

"I'm sorry, did we have a meeting scheduled?" Her voice was sharp with an accent I couldn't place.

"No, but I was hoping you could share something about your charity's work. A friend is one of your donors and she recommended the foundation to me."

"Oh, who is that?"

"Victoria Hartman," I replied, mentally crossing my fingers against the lie.

"Ms. Hartman is your friend?"

"Unfortunately, Victoria passed away a few weeks ago." I expected some showing of shock or sympathy, but Andrea Faber was stone-faced. I plowed on. "I understand the foundation focuses on helping children."

Seeming to remember her role, or perhaps recognizing me for the first time as a potential contributor, she gave a tight smile and nodded. "We partner with various organizations that provide assistance to children from impoverished backgrounds: activity centers, mentoring services, and similar support agencies."

"Like the Oreola Children's Center?"

"That is one of the agencies we fund."

"I was wondering if Victoria had an interest in a particular aspect of your work, or in one of your collaborators."

The frost descended again. "Ms. Hartman did not tell you?"

"Tell me what?" I said, trying for innocent, but my comeback was too fast.

"If she is—was—your friend, did she not tell you what drew her to the foundation?"

I gave a helpless shrug. "Well, maybe you could give me some literature that describes the organizations you work with, and I can see which one speaks to me." I suspected she had seen through my pretense of being a wealthy philanthropist. I wondered if the jeans and T-shirt had given me away.

"Of course." Ms. Faber walked over to one of the other desks and selected a few brochures. She handed me the pile, the Oreola Children's Center leaflet on top. She remained standing, indicating my time was up. I stood too.

"Oh, by the way, do you know Gaston Lemesur?" I threw the question over my shoulder, pausing to assess her reaction. She was silent. She could have been searching her memory for the name—I couldn't tell from her expression.

"No." She was implacable.

I decided to push it: what did I have to lose? "Really? That's surprising."

Bingo! She shot an involuntary glance at the file cabinets. "We have a duty of privacy to our clients—I mean the clients of our partner organizations. I can tell you nothing."

Ah, Andrea, but you have. "And who was the charming lad who opened the door to me?"

But the drawbridge was up. "I can tell you nothing," she repeated as she hustled me into the street.

As I hunched into a keen wind, I placed Andrea Faber's accent: French.

****

Back in my room at the hotel, after a late lunch at an overpriced burger joint next door, I considered my morning's discoveries. Perhaps the key to the mystery was not the inheritance after all; perhaps it was Gaston Lemesur and his connection to the foundation. Silencing the nagging voice that said there was no mystery and therefore no key, and I should stick to my resolution to wind this investigation up, I picked up my phone and started googling. I was sure the expert heir tracers at Stein Pinter had more sophisticated tools at their disposal when they tried to track down the missing beneficiary, but perhaps they had missed something.

Google turned up nothing, and neither did Facebook. Perhaps Gaston was more the TikTok generation: *nada*. I tried a couple more of the trendier social media sites with no success. Maybe he was a professional type? LinkedIn had no user named Gaston Lemesur. I knew Instagram was owned by Facebook, so I suspected that a search of one would have turned up the other site's users but decided to give it a try anyway. I typed in the full name and was offered a selection of Gastons with various last names that did not resemble Lemesur. I scrolled through them as I had on the other sites, almost missing Glemesur. The profile picture was a gray silhouette: the user had not uploaded a profile picture. I tapped on it. Glemesur had two followers. He was following eighty-five accounts. His own account was private and I'd have to follow him to gain access to his photos and videos. Could this be Gaston? I sent a request to follow, not feeling hopeful. Someone with only two followers was either pretty picky about who he let into his world, or just didn't use the app much—or was dead. I pushed that last thought aside in favor of optimism: seeing my request, maybe he'd try to follow me to find out who I was, and I could connect that way. But maybe Glemesur wasn't Gaston Lemesur after all. The nagging voice—John's voice—was hissing at me again.

I stretched out on the bed with the British murder mystery I'd purchased. Soon I was strolling the gritty Glasgow streets in the company of a battered misanthropic detective who pissed off all his superiors in the force. I felt right at home.

Chapter 7

Back at work, I was thrust into a new case: financial fraud. We knew the perp, but the captain wanted the evidence nailed down before we applied for an arrest warrant. That meant days of trawling through data: phone records, bank statements, CCTV video. Long hours of tedious, mind-numbing work for which I was grateful: it distracted me from thinking about Victoria.

I had not heard from John since he'd made good on his promise to pick me up the previous Friday at the airport and take me to lunch. We'd gone to a cozy restaurant up the coast. The weather was mild for November, and after some excellent seafood and a bottle of white wine, we took a stroll along the waterfront—all very relaxing. We did not discuss my Philadelphia trip, other than John inquiring politely about my flight and whether the time change bothered me.

I told myself I was relieved he had not called. Knowing he disapproved of my investigation into Victoria's life cast a shadow over our relationship. But I still wanted to justify my Philly adventure, tell him about the leads I'd developed, the questions still unanswered.

"Relationship" might overstate what we had. We'd taken baby steps in that direction since first bonding over Victoria's dead body. We hadn't kissed or anything yet, although I thought that maybe this was where we were headed before I left for Philadelphia. I hadn't visited his house out in the county, and he'd only come up to my apartment once for a quick drink before we went to a movie. John was ten years older than me and had never been married, although a passing comment led me to believe he'd had a long-term live-in partner at some point. I didn't inquire further. Other than the necessary, rent-splitting roommate, I'd never shared my living space as an adult, and I wasn't in a hurry to do so. Regular, uncomplicated sex would be nice, but I sensed that John wasn't in that market. He was a serious man, thoughtful about other people's feelings. Even though his "patients" were all dead, he approached them with a respect that contrasted with other medical examiners I'd had contact with. I wasn't ready for the kind of commitment John might expect from a girlfriend, that is, if he wanted a girlfriend and hadn't decided to back away from the crazy bitch he was beginning to think I was.

Staying busy was the best way of not thinking about John too.

When, on Tuesday morning, Captain Kleinberg summoned me into his office, I assumed he was now satisfied that we had our ducks in a row and he was going to green-light the arrest. Bill Kleinberg and I were not pals. He hadn't wanted to promote me to sergeant, saying I was "not a team player." By that he meant I didn't like football or hang out drinking with him and the other (male) detectives. But there'd been an open spot, I had seniority, and he couldn't argue with my solve rate.

He didn't invite me to sit, which wasn't unusual. He was concentrating on some papers in front of him, bullish head thrust forward and meaty hands resting on the desk. I waited.

"We've had a complaint," he announced, frowning

up at me.

That didn't alarm me. We were always getting complaints—from old ladies who thought we took too long to respond to their 911 calls about a missing kitty, or helicopter parents objecting to us breathalyzing their under-age kids when they crashed their dads' sports cars.

"What were you doing in Philadelphia last week?" he growled.

"I was on leave. I'm from that area." Who'd snitched? I ran through the list of those I'd given my card to, telling myself to keep calm although I could feel color rising to my cheeks.

"You conducted an interrogation outside this jurisdiction without obtaining the local department's permission—or mine! And into a closed case! You could lose your job over this." He was shouting, enjoying himself. "You picked the wrong man with Jerome Pinter." He continued. "He's friends with the Philadelphia police commissioner, who sits on a committee with our chief. So I got a call from the chief last night at home, wanting to know what the hell you were playing at."

"Do I need my union rep here?" I asked. I didn't want to get fired: my job was my life. I wished I'd never gone to Philadelphia.

Kleinberg hesitated, weighing something in his mind. "Not yet. I want to hear your story—all of it. Then I'll decide what disciplinary action needs to be taken."

This sounded hopeful. The captain would like nothing better than to fire me on the spot, but I suspected he'd been made aware of the political consequences by the higher-ups. Firing the only female detective in the squad wouldn't look good.

"First of all, it wasn't an interrogation. I went to Pinter's law firm to tie up some employment details—just background stuff that had worried me. I thought the case had been closed prematurely; there were so many odd circumstances. I asked to speak to the office manager and Pinter came and sat in on the meeting. In fact, they asked for my help in finding Victoria Hartman's insurance beneficiary. It was all very friendly. I never said I was there on behalf of the Department."

"Jesus Christ! You gave him your business card! Of course he thought you were there officially!"

I let out a deep breath. "Okay, what can I do to make it right? I'll email him an apology: 'regret if I left the wrong impression' kind of thing."

"It'll need to be stronger than that, a full apology, and attach a copy of the autopsy report."

"What?"

He pretended to have lost interest, back to staring at his paperwork. "Yeah, Pinter needs a copy—something to do with insurance, I expect."

"But he has the official cause of death. What does he need the complete report for? Are we even allowed to give out—"

"McQuarry, I've had enough! Do you want to keep your job? Then send an apology and attach the report. Run the wording by me first."

As I walked back to my desk, I felt the eyes of the rest of the squad on me. Were my cheeks still red? Had they heard the shouting and were already plotting to take my job?

"So, is it a go?" asked one of the detectives who had been pulling overtime on the fraud case. I realized with relief that the other guys assumed, as I had, that the captain was reviewing the sufficiency of the evidence.

"No, not yet." I hunkered down behind my computer monitor, pushing my paranoia behind me. I wanted to get the damn apology over with, but before I started drafting, I retrieved the Hartman file from archives and located the autopsy report. As I opened it on my screen, I remembered reading the executive summary on the first page and only skimming the rest. The summary contained gender, age, general condition of the body, and the cause of death—drug overdose. The evidence that supported the COD was listed, along with any exceptional aspects—in Victoria's case, her rare blood type and the PNH blood disease. The body of the report, which I now scrolled to, described the particulars of the autopsy process and the pathologist's detailed findings. John's report was meticulous. He had gone over every inch of Victoria's body. The blood analysis alone took up more than a page of—to me—unintelligible ranges and values.

Why on earth did Pinter want the full autopsy report? I doubted he needed it for insurance purposes. A death certificate should have been enough for that. Did he suspect foul play? Victoria's position as law firm administrator might have given her access to confidential client information. If she'd threatened to leak sensitive secrets, someone might have a motive for silencing her. Pure speculation, I knew. Still, Pinter had to have a reason. Had John missed something? Unlikely. I pulled a notebook and pen towards me and began reading with care.

At the end of half an hour, three bullet points stared up at me from my notes. First, John mentioned a recent needle mark on the inside of Victoria's elbow. He commented that the mark was consistent with a regular blood draw to monitor her illness. Perhaps. It might also be consistent with an injection of some fast-acting drug, something that knocked her out and then disappeared from her system by the time she died. I ached to call John and explore this possibility with him but knew that would be a serious mistake. The fact I was even reading the report would confirm his opinion that I had become morbidly fixated on Victoria Hartman.

Second, there was a discoloration on her upper left arm, about two centimeters wide and three centimeters long. The report stated that the mark was a healing hematoma, maybe a day or two old, and again referenced Victoria's PNH disease: a side effect was a tendency to bruise easily. Sure, but something or someone had to have caused the bruise in the first place.

Third, John described how he had cleaned under her fingernails, a routine check for foreign DNA that might have been deposited if Victoria had fought off an attacker. No DNA material was found. *Nothing* was found. Her nail beds were immaculate, sterile even. How strange to take care to scour under your nails after presumably ingesting a death-dealing dose of drugs. John made no comment on this odd finding.

Kleinberg exited his office and made in my direction. Like a guilty schoolchild, I closed the autopsy document and went back to my draft email. He stopped in the middle of the squad room. "Right. We're ready to get the warrant."

I started to stand.

"Not you." He pointed at the detective who had spoken up when I left the captain's office. "Myers, gather the paperwork and call Judge Freeman." To me:

"You carry on with that other thing."

I finished my craven apology, hoping Pinter would read the sarcasm beneath my flowery phrases—and that the captain wouldn't. I sent the email to the boss for review. He responded with a terse "Send it." I located Pinter's email address, attached the autopsy report and fired it off.

It was past five p.m. The arrest warrant wouldn't be executed until the next morning. Before I left for the day, I opened the top drawer of my desk and extracted the photo of Victoria retained from that day a few weeks ago when I had searched for her in the missing person reports. I slid the photo and my notes on the autopsy into a manila folder, and put the folder into my backpack under the desk. "See y'all tomorrow bright and early!" I called out to the remaining detectives in the room, receiving a few grunts and waves in response. I had a busy evening at home ahead of me.

****

I poured myself a glass of red wine and grabbed a handful of almonds; supper could wait until I'd made a start on my murder board. Every murder investigation begins with a white board in the incident room. The victim's photo is placed at the center top, and, as suspects or material witnesses are identified, their photos are added. I didn't have a white board in my apartment, but the small second bedroom I used as an office had one bare white wall, and I had sticky notes and scotch tape.

I taped up Victoria's picture, and stood contemplating her face, marshaling my thoughts. Then I leaped into action, scribbling names on sticky note after sticky note and arranging them on either side of the victim: Dr. Luchinski, Frances Bell, Jerome Pinter, Ruth

Romano, Andrea Faber, Gaston Lemesur. I even wrote one for Arun Shah, the new tenant in Victoria's apartment, but decided his connection was too remote, balled up the note and tossed it on the floor.

Lower down on the wall and to one side, I placed cryptic notes that represented lines of inquiry: inheritance from father? Competing claims? Law firm secrets? Change of beneficiary? Ditton Foundation—clients and partner orgs? I also taped up my page of autopsy notes. I stepped back and surveyed the wall, dissatisfied. It was a mess: lots of questions and no likelihood of getting answers with all witnesses off-limits and a continent's width away.

After more thought, I wrote another note: mugging—was I a target?

I drank a second glass of wine while I waited for my frozen pizza to heat. And another while I chowed down two slices. What remained in the bottle didn't seem worth saving so I poured it into my glass. The frustration I'd felt surveying my murder wall—so many unanswerable questions—was now overlaid with a "fuck 'em all" buzz. I picked up the Glasgow detective novel I'd bought in Philadelphia and stretched out on the sofa.

I woke at 2:15 a.m. with a snail's trail of drool down my chin and a mouth like the floor of a parrot's cage. I remembered too late that red wine acted as a depressant for me. After I dumped the rest of the pizza in the garbage, I turned off lights and headed for the bathroom.

Enough ambient light penetrated from the bathroom window for me to see a shadowy figure in there, a pale face outlined by darkness. My heart jumped into my throat: it was Victoria! Her eyes stared into mine—her expression seemed reproachful, almost accusatory; she didn't blink. I must have frozen for some seconds before I was able to scramble for the light switch.

In the sudden glare, the mirror over the sink opposite the bathroom door reflected my white face, the blue hollows under my eyes, tousled dark hair, the black turtleneck. I let out a weak laugh: I'd been frightened by my own ghost. It unsettled me though, and I found it difficult to get back to sleep. The bedclothes wound around my legs like tree roots, my pillow was stuffed with rocks, and the pizza was giving me heartburn. The knowledge that I had to be at work by seven a.m. to organize the service of the arrest warrant didn't help.

At some point, I fell into one of those shallow dreams where you're at home in your own bed but things have shifted. I was looking out into space where the wall of the room should be. Far below was a raging torrent of water and the green canopy of a forest. I looked to my left; what should have been the wall of the apartment building was a rock ledge. Victoria was standing about ten feet along, staring out into the void. I wanted to call out to her to be careful, she could fall, but the words were stuck in my mouth like pebbles. I tried to free my arms from the bedclothes to gesture to her, to no avail. She turned to look at me, the same accusing gaze I'd seen in the bathroom mirror, then she stepped forward.

I woke to the sickening sensation of falling. The dream was still vivid. Was it Victoria on that ledge or me? Was I the one who deliberately plunged off to certain death? Had we changed places in the night, and now I was dead and she was trying to find out why? Doppelgänger: the word flashed into my brain from nowhere—or from my subconscious. I couldn't remember ever hearing the word, but I knew what it meant. Victoria and I were doppelgängers: identical but unrelated. Parallel existences that had collided. It felt mystical, sinister.

Now fully conscious, I pushed the dream away. I had no patience for the supernatural. There was no doubt a scientific explanation, a Wikipedia page that described the phenomenon of doppelgänger in terms of genomes and probabilities. I promised myself I'd do some research. More urgently, I had to shower, dress, and go to work. And deal with this hangover.

Chapter 8

The handsome middle-aged man who opened the door seemed prepared for us. He was neatly groomed and dressed in a suit, white shirt and silk tie; he listened politely as I read him his rights. His wife and teenage daughter stumbled down the stairs, still in their nightclothes, faces bleary with sleep, confused at first, then tearful.

"Call my lawyer. The number's next to the bed," he called out, over their protests and questions.

His attorney was already at the front desk when we arrived back at the police department. He didn't need to advise his client to remain silent: the fraudster had not uttered another word since leaving his house. There followed a frustrating interview where every legal interrogation technique failed to get him to even say yes to a cup of coffee. At eleven a.m., we sent him down to the cells and handed the case over to the prosecutor's office.

I was at a loose end. The adrenalin rush that had kept me going all morning had receded, leaving me with a dull headache and a queasy stomach. I needed caffeine and some solid food. As I left the station house, I ran into John coming in.

"Hey, I was hoping to see you." He seemed cheerful, friendly. I reminded myself it had only been five days since we'd had lunch; in spite of my imaginings, he had not shunned me. "Early lunch?"

"Yes, I'd love to," I replied, feeling better already.

Once we were seated in front of our chicken Caesar salads—John drank water, I had a super-sized caffeine-rich soda—he asked me what I was doing for Thanksgiving.

"Oh, my God, is that next week?" I had lost track of the calendar; the dreaded holidays were almost here. "Well, if I'm not on duty, I'll be curling up with a good book and take-out Thai food, as usual."

"How about coming to my place? Nothing fancy, but I enjoy cooking the traditional meal, and I can't eat a whole turkey by myself. A couple of neighbors will be there too."

I took my time chewing a mouthful, trying to parse the nuances of the invitation. What the hell, maybe he actually did enjoy cooking for company. I'd rather have root canal surgery than slave in the kitchen for five hours, but man—or woman—cannot live by frozen pizza alone. I was pleased to be included in John's plans. "Yes, I'd love to. What can I bring? Please say a bottle of wine—I can't cook."

He laughed. "Why am I not surprised! Listen, bring a pie for dessert. Just go to the grocery store and buy one. No one will care."

****

In the end I bought two pies: pecan and apple. And a can of whipped cream to squirt over them to disguise the fact that Marie Callender had done all the work. Plus a bottle of wine, because—well, just because.

John lived about half an hour from town in an old farmhouse that he was gradually restoring. He'd started with the invisible but essential structural work—

mending roof leaks and putting in new wiring—leaving the cosmetic stuff until later. He had renovated the kitchen though, from which emanated the mouthwatering smell of roasting turkey. The other guests were a gay couple—retired from jobs in the film industry in Los Angeles to purchase "the spread" next door and reinvent themselves as gentlemen farmers— and their twitchy teenage niece.

After introductions were made, I followed John into the kitchen to hand over my contribution to the feast.

"I'll put these to warm in the oven when I take the turkey out," he said, stripping the pies of their branded boxes. "No one will ever know your secret. I should warn you: Britney is in recovery. She's staying with Perry and Ed to keep her away from temptation in the city. It's this or back into rehab. She's not happy about it."

I gestured at the wine I'd brought. "Should I hide this then?"

"Drugs are her problem, not alcohol. There's already a bottle of red open. Help yourself."

I gave myself a generous pour and took a gulp to quell my nervousness. I had little confidence in my social skills—lack of practice, I guess. I needn't have worried: Perry and Ed were accountants not actors, but they had a stream of semi-scandalous stories about movie celebrities that kept us entertained throughout dinner. John and I needed only to provide the occasional prompt to launch another anecdote, which was good as neither forensic pathology nor crime make for jolly holiday conversation.

Britney ate little and said less. She stared at her food as if it offended her, declined dessert and started scrolling on her phone.

"No phones at the table, dear," said Ed gently, with an apologetic glance at the rest of us. Britney sighed and looked daggers at her uncles, but complied. Her pouting presence cast a pall over the rest of the meal, and as soon as they had helped clear the dishes, Perry and Ed made their excuses and took Britney home.

"Come sit down. There's still some wine left." John put another log on the fire and invited me to join him on the sofa. With just one table lamp on, the peeling wallpaper and scarred floors faded into the background, leaving us in an island of firelight. We sat staring into the flames, full of good food. I was relaxed, at home in the shabbiness and silence.

I felt John's eyes on me and I turned to face him. There was no mistaking the message. We started to kiss, softly at first, then with more urgency. He pulled me against him, his arms tight around my body. I felt the size and strength of him, smelled his skin, still infused with cooking aromas. We both knew where this was headed, and we wanted it.

John put his hands on my shoulders and held me inches away from his face, his eyes searching mine. A faint warning bell sounded in some recess of my brain.

"Christine, are you ready for this?"

My voice sounded hoarse with desire. "Yes, I'm ready." I leaned forward to kiss him again, but he kept his hold, a slight frown puckering his forehead.

"I mean, you're all done with that other thing?"

The bell was deafening now. Victoria. He meant Victoria. He was pitting himself against Victoria. I could have him or her, but not both. I moved away from him to resume staring into the fire while I processed John's question. As a picture of my murder wall flashed into my head—all those lines of inquiry—any sexual urge drained from my body. Instead, there was a heaviness in my chest. I had to be careful how I responded. When I thought I could control my voice, I turned back to him with a forced smile.

"Well, I thought I was all done when I got back from Philly, but then Victoria's employer requested a complete copy of the autopsy report. He obviously thinks something's wrong."

"That's ridiculous!" John stood abruptly and gave the fire an unnecessary poke. Our moment had passed, and he couldn't look at me. "I'm trained to search for any possible sign of a suspicious death. I've done hundreds of autopsies in my career. Do you honestly think I would have missed signs of foul play?"

I shrugged, watching John carefully.

His professional expertise had been impugned; he was angry. Or was there something else? I knew he and Victoria's doctor, Dr. Luchinski, had spoken more than once about the case. Perhaps John's findings had been influenced by the other doctor's comments, for example, about taking regular blood draws to explain the needle mark on Victoria's arm.

I decided against raising this, or the other points I'd gleaned from reading the autopsy report. And I certainly wasn't going to tell him about Frances Bell's theories, Andrea Faber's strange hostility, or the French connection to the missing beneficiary.

I finished my wine. "This has been so great, but I'm on duty tomorrow, an early start." I stretched, then stood too. "I love your house, and the meal was fantastic. Let's do lunch next week sometime."

John recovered himself and resumed his role as host,

offering me leftovers to take home, fetching my coat, making sure I felt sober enough to drive. At the door, I reached up to kiss his cheek. He didn't recoil, but didn't respond either. "Tell Perry and Ed how much I enjoyed meeting them. I do hope everything goes okay with Britney. And thanks again."

John raised a hand in farewell. I wondered whether we'd be able to resume our previous friendly professional relationship. I guessed we would. He was too buttoned-up to explore an emotional injury, assuming I'd had the power to inflict one, and too self-assured to examine whether he'd been at fault.

Once I was outside the circle cast by the porch light, I stopped and looked up at the sky. It was a clear night, no moon. This far from town, a gazillion stars pierced the blackness. The Milky Way's smear bisected the heavens. I knew that many of the bright pinpricks I saw were already extinguished, imploded into black holes in space. Like Victoria Hartman: dead but still streaming a beam of light.

I should be angry or disappointed. Instead I felt a vague sense of relief. John had turned out to be the same kind of controlling guy I'd come across in the past—the type who knew what was best for me, who wanted to fix me. What if I didn't want fixing? What if I didn't *need* fixing? I was on my own again and that felt good. I didn't have to avoid certain subjects, or cater to someone else's ego.

Before I got into my car, I took a last look up at the stars, trying to wrap my brain around the distance their light had traveled. I was more than ever determined to trace Victoria's singular light back to its source, to understand her life and death, no matter what it took.

Chapter 9

John realized he could have handled it differently. His history with Nancy should have warned him not to try and change another person's behavior. But now he was more than intrigued by Christine: he was strongly attracted to her. He wanted her in his life. She was charming at dinner, great with Perry and Ed—even with their sulky niece. Afterwards, finishing the wine by firelight, was the perfect moment. John was hot for her and she responded with equal passion. He couldn't quite remember what he said. His intention was to tell her that it wasn't just physical but that he cared for her, wanted her to stop worrying about Victoria, to be happy, for them to be happy together.

"Victoria's employer has asked for a copy of the autopsy report. He thinks something's wrong," she said. It was like a sheet of ice falling between them.

John had blown up. She was impugning his professional reputation, suggesting his autopsy findings were incorrect. After all the consideration he had shown for her and her craziness. No wonder she was distrusted by her colleagues. Did John call her ridiculous? That was a mistake. She left almost at once.

As the door closed behind her, John turned toward the kitchen, his anger ebbing into regret. He should have probed exactly what Victoria's employer had said. They could have discussed the autopsy report like adults. The problem was they'd both drunk too much wine. Should he call the next day and apologize? No, he'd wait a few days for her to call. Maybe she'd get in touch just to say thanks for the meal. That would give him an opening—not for an apology, but some gesture of understanding.

He missed her already.

Chapter 10

At work the following week, I kept my head down, arriving early and leaving on time. I avoided Kleinberg and didn't make waves with my colleagues. Each night I hurried home to my murder wall, stopping only to buy a heat-and-eat meal and a bottle of wine. It was frustrating not being able to use the federal databases, surveillance videos and other law enforcement computer tools at my disposal in the office, but I'd had one brush with discipline and didn't want another, so I was limited to browsing the web and social media on my own laptop in the evening.

It was surprising what you could find out. Dr. Luchinski, for example, had volunteered with *Médecins Sans Frontières* in Bosnia in the early nineties. He had begun to specialize in blood diseases after his return to the States. An adjunct professor at the University of Pennsylvania's School of Medicine, he also served on the board of a charity clinic for children. The clinic name sounded familiar, sending me rooting through my file folder. I found a leaflet describing the place, one of several Andrea Faber had handed me as representative of agencies supported by the Ditton Foundation. Not exactly an "Aha!" moment, but another connection in the opaque tangle of Victoria's past.

What I really needed was a partner on the ground in Philadelphia to dig deeper and ask the follow-up questions. Luchinski wouldn't work: my trust in him had been compromised by his side conversations with John. (John had tried to reach me—I'd seen his number flash up on my phone—but I didn't accept the call, and he didn't leave a voicemail. So I guess, in his words, that was that.) Ruth Romano, the law firm administrator, was sympathetic, but she wouldn't want to risk her job, and anyway her priority was taking care of her family in the suburbs. That left Frances Bell, the drama queen and narcissist: not a reliable witness. So I was stuck with the internet and sticky notes.

I'd switched to white wine in the evenings, but my sleep—when I finally nodded off—was still troubled by dreams in which I was an anxious observer of some nebulous tragedy I could not prevent. I knew I was drinking too much and eating crap. I hadn't been for a run since before my Philadelphia trip, or even climbed on the stationary bike. I resolved to shape up as soon as all this was over. I might even try a dating app again: somewhere *I* could control the narrative.

But would "all this" ever be over? Victoria had become part of me, hovering at the back of my mind even when I was working on something else. I couldn't imagine a time when I would forget about her. The puzzle of her death—why she died here—was one thing; I would solve it or not. My relationship to her was another; regardless of DNA, she was the sister I never had. Through her, I could reimagine my childhood. She would have been my ally against my parents, my confidante and friend. With her by my side, I would have grown into a more complete adult.

My parents didn't beat me or starve me. I couldn't complain to the authorities that they abused me. They just ignored me. They were so wrapped up in each other that they didn't want children. Theirs was a passionate, tempestuous marriage. They quarreled violently, I think for the ecstasy of making up. They drank to excess, each blaming the other for driving them to it. One night, when their arguing woke me, my mother noticed me peering through the banisters.

"Wha' you lookin' at, you li'l worm? I shoulda aborted you when I had the chance!"

My father just grinned sloppily up from the armchair where he was sprawled. "Atta girl!" he said, whether to her or me, I couldn't tell.

A precocious eight-year-old, I looked up "abort" in the big dictionary at the library. After that, I concentrated on being invisible, pretending that I *had* been aborted and was now a ghost, able to move through the world without being touched, detached from other humans and the hurt they inflicted. Occasionally, my pretense collapsed and suppressed rage broke through, like the time I punched out that girl at school.

Then my parents drove into a highway bridge abutment on a rainy night when I was sixteen. By then they'd destroyed other bridges, alienating friends and family in their fiery obsession with each other: my isolation was complete. My parents should have died sooner, when there might still be time to recover some of my childhood, but at sixteen the shell had hardened around my heart. Victoria was the first person to crack it.

One morning—a week after the Thanksgiving fiasco—I had a call at work from an unknown number with a 215 prefix. I recognized the Philadelphia area code.

"McQuarry." I used my gruffest voice, not getting my hopes up. It was probably a robocall.

"Good afternoon, Detective Sergeant McQuarry—but it's probably still morning there. Jerome Pinter. I thought I'd call to see how your inquiries into Victoria Hartman are going."

I stared at the phone in my hand. Pinter was the last person I expected to hear from. Hadn't he tried to get me fired? Whatever his motive for contacting me, it was bound to be devious. I needed to play this carefully. "I've been instructed to go no further in my investigation," I responded after a pause.

"Really? And you've obeyed instructions? I didn't think you were the sort of woman to give up so easily!" He chuckled, pretending a friendliness I didn't trust for a minute.

"How can I help you, sir?" I considered hanging up but thought that might provoke another complaint. I'd just be my most professional self.

"Well, it's more how I can help you, Christine—may I call you Christine? Detective Sergeant McQuarry's rather a mouthful."

I didn't answer. While I waited for him to say more, I glanced around the squad room. A knot of detectives was gathered around a computer screen. I heard the captain's voice from the corridor as he approached.

Pinter continued, "A week ago I received a call from a local attorney, James Anderson. He represented Victoria's father and handled the probate of his estate." This was useful information; I'd wanted to find the man who might know more about Victoria's legacy and the possible competing claims. But there was more. "He also drafted Victoria's will just a few weeks before she died.

I thought you might be interested in hearing what was in it."

Kleinberg was now waving us all into group; he had something important to say.

"I might be, but right now I'm being called into a meeting, so—"

"I can send a copy, if you like. I have your email address."

"No!" I blurted out. He had my police department email; I didn't want Victoria's will coming here. "Send it to this email address." I spelled out my personal account. "I have to go."

"I'll be in touch, then."

I disconnected and hurried over to where the boss was briefing the squad. "We have a hostage situation."

****

It was after eight p.m. when I got home. The Department has a detailed protocol for hostage situations. The hostage negotiator, the SWAT team, and uniformed officers handle the incident scene, while detectives work feverishly to uncover as much background as possible on the suspect, the hostages, the building in which they're being held and its surroundings, and relay it to the personnel at the scene. On this occasion, a plan of the premises—a jewelry store—showed an obscure back entrance to the basement. The SWAT team got into position there while the negotiator persuaded the suspect to release the two store employees he was holding in exchange for a getaway car to be pulled up in front. All this took hours of back and forth, pleas from the suspect's mother, and even a pizza delivery to the people trapped in the store. After dramatic footage aired on the six o'clock news, the suspect gave in, the employees staggered out into the floodlit street, and the SWAT team entered through the back, setting off a smoke bomb which allowed them to apprehend the hostage-taker without a shot being fired.

I ducked out of the celebratory beerfest and rushed back to my apartment. I logged onto the computer and accessed my email account. Pinter's message was terse: *This should help you find Gaston Lemesur.* I double-clicked on the attachment, Victoria's last will and testament. After some dense legal preamble, I reached the meat of the document on the second page:

"After payment of my just debts, funeral expenses, and expenses of my last illness, I direct that my residuary estate be distributed to my son, Gaston Lemesur of Montreal, Province of Quebec, Canada, date of birth January 11, 2002."

This was a major development. Frances Bell had speculated about a love child. She had been partly right: the secret baby was Victoria's own, not a sibling. I did the math in my head: Victoria had been seventeen when she gave birth to Gaston, and he was now also aged seventeen. A hundred questions rushed through my mind: Who was the father? How much was Victoria's residuary estate worth? Had Gaston been given up for adoption, just as Victoria had been? Had she only recently reconnected with him, which spurred her to make her will, but also gave her a strong reason not to kill herself? Maybe the fresh start she'd told Frances about was with her son? Perhaps most puzzling: Why did Pinter share a copy of the will with me? Surely, with this precise information, he'd have no difficulty locating the boy and discharging his duty to distribute the proceeds of Victoria's 401k and life insurance. James Anderson had probably made contact already.

I read on, hoping for clarification. The will provided that if Gaston was a minor at the time of Victoria's death—he was—the estate was to be placed in trust until his twenty-first birthday. The trustee was Victoria's executor, James Anderson, and the trust could only be encroached on to pay educational expenses at a college or university in the United States of America and associated living expenses.

The time on the East Coast was eleven thirty p.m., far too late to call Jerome Pinter, and I only had his office number anyway. I set my alarm for five a.m. hoping, like me, he arrived at the office early.

****

"Anderson came to me because he can't find any trace of a Gaston Lemesur in Montreal," Jerome Pinter explained when I reached him in his office the next morning. "When he discussed the will with Victoria, she led him to assume she was in contact with her son. He never thought to ask for an address or phone number. Besides, she was only thirty-five years old; he didn't anticipate he'd be searching for heirs in a matter of weeks."

"What about you? Has your firm tried to find him in Montreal?"

"Yes, with no luck either. I don't think he's living in Montreal." He paused. I listened to the silence; he was deciding how much to tell me. I didn't trust the man; from our first meeting, he'd been playing with hidden cards, manipulating information for no good reason that I could see. "That's why I thought we could work together. Locating the boy might help answer your questions about why she came to your town to die...and *how* she died."

"It was a drug overdose." I wasn't going to play his game.

"But the autopsy can't tell us if it was accidental, suicide or…" If he was going to suggest murder, he'd have to say the word out loud; I wasn't going to help. He took another direction. "Victoria wrote a letter to Gaston and left it in Anderson's hands along with the will. It's a fairly common practice. The law prevents testators from imposing certain conditions on a legacy from beyond the grave. It's called the Dead Hand Rule. But they can write a letter expressing those wishes outside the will, and it often has persuasive effect."

"Fascinating," I said dryly.

"The contents of the letter might offer clues as to where Gaston is living and with whom. The problem is, it's sealed. Anderson feels we shouldn't open it."

I began to see where this was heading. "But you feel differently." I could almost hear him squirming.

"As a lawyer and an officer of the court, I must adhere meticulously to the letter of the law, even in exigent circumstances like these." His vocabulary had escalated along with his discomfort. "I have the reputation of the firm to consider, as well as my own." Whereas I had no reputation to protect and had already proved myself ready to cut corners to obtain information. I wanted to laugh.

"How much are we talking about here? I mean Gaston's legacy?"

"About two and a half million dollars, plus another half million from the 401k and life insurance."

I whistled. "Three million provides a strong motive for murder." Damn, I'd said the word aloud. I hadn't wanted to give Pinter any encouragement.

"That assumes Lemesur knew about the inheritance—knew who his birth mother was."

We were both silent for a while, thinking the scenario through. It appeared that Victoria only rediscovered her son a short time ago, prompting her to change the beneficiary of her employee benefits and to make a will. That suggested that Gaston might have been living in Montreal at one time but had since disappeared. If she hadn't yet taken the step of contacting him, she may have placed him there in her will acting on outdated information.

"Adoption records," I declared. "Victoria knew how to research them because she'd tried to find her own birth parents. She must have found her own son's adoption record while she was searching."

"Yes, my people are trying to get that information, but it's difficult. There are privacy restrictions; the agencies won't release information to anyone other than birth mother and child."

"Even when the mother is dead?" I asked. I had another thought. "Perhaps it was a private adoption, done unofficially without recording it." That's how Victoria's parents had adopted her. Perhaps they pushed their seventeen-year-old daughter down the same route.

"We could just wait for Lemesur to come forward." Pinter sounded hesitant. Where was this "we" coming from?

"Hmm, assuming that he knows about his birth mother, the will, and that she's dead." I needed time to think through where all this was leading. "Anyway, I have to get to work—my *real* work. Good luck with finding Gaston. Keep me posted." I disconnected before he could object. The first thing I wanted to do was have a conversation with James Anderson. He was named as the executor of Victoria's will and I should have no problem finding him. He would have first-hand information about Victoria's state of mind, what she knew and didn't know, what she was planning. He had the family history too, having represented Victoria's father.

I started jotting down questions when I noticed the time. I did still have a real job, and I didn't want to be late for it.

Chapter 11

I was working on a big drug case involving several law enforcement agencies: the DEA, the state bureau of investigation, and even the RCMP in Canada because that's where significant amounts of fentanyl were coming from. We'd nabbed a few low-level dealers but had no luck linking them to the big fish. The captain hated the case because he wasn't in charge; I loved it for the same reason. With so many agencies participating, I had the freedom to follow my own lines of investigation independently. Of course, I was supposed to enter all my activities in the joint task force database, but I could always do that after the fact and reframe the entry to show off the results of my inquiries. If anyone asked where I was going or who I was meeting, I'd say, "Oh, just following up on a suggestion the DEA made," or, "The Canadians need this ASAP."

So when I left the office for the night, I mumbled something about checking in with an undercover guy the next morning and I might be late. I wanted to give myself plenty of time to talk to James Anderson, hoping I could reach him first thing. My research showed that Anderson was in his mid-sixties, a solo practitioner who specialized in "elder law"—wills and guardianships. He'd obtained his JD at Rutgers Law School, and worked for a couple of smallish law firms before going solo about a dozen years ago. His folksy website showed a white-haired geezer thigh-deep in a trout stream, noted that he was a collector of Depression-era glassware, and his labrador retriever was called Sandy. I set the alarm for five thirty a.m.

****

"Christine McQuarry? Yes, Jerome Pinter mentioned you might call. Aren't you the police officer that found Victoria Hartman's body?" James Anderson had answered his office phone himself when I called on the dot of nine eastern. He assured me he had plenty of time to talk.

"Actually, I was the detective charged with finding out the identity of a Jane Doe. I didn't find the body," I explained. "And it was the Medical Examiner who identified Victoria in the end by tracking down her doctor. I'm calling because I thought you might have some information about Victoria's plans—how she ended up here in Washington?"

"No idea, but I can tell you this: I was astounded to hear she'd died of a drug overdose. That doesn't sound like Victoria at all."

I felt a smile spread across my face; this guy had opinions and he wasn't reluctant to share them. "The overdose might have been accidental..." I ventured.

"I doubt it. Victoria was a careful sort of person. And as for suicide, when I last saw her she was in good spirits. I don't believe she would have killed herself."

"When did you last see her?"

"On September 28th." His response was prompt. "She came in to sign her will and to leave a letter to be opened by her son in the event of her death—" which happened about two weeks later. "Look, I'd better tell you the whole story. I first met Victoria's parents about

74

fifteen years ago when I helped them with their wills. These were what we call mirror wills: each left everything to the other, and after they both passed, then it all went to the daughter. As far as I remember, Ted and Joan didn't have a great deal besides the house. Ted was an insurance sales agent, and Joan was a homemaker."

I was content to let Anderson fill me in on the background, even if it seemed irrelevant. Anderson was eager to talk. He'd get to Victoria eventually.

"Joan died in 2013, I believe," he continued. "Then last year, Ted came to see me. He wanted to make a new will in Victoria's favor. I told him it was unnecessary: his existing will had provided for Joan's earlier death, and Victoria would inherit everything anyway, but he insisted. He wanted specific language in there with her full name and date of birth. Ted had cancer—he'd been told he only had a few months. I humored him—I wasn't about to turn away business. That's when he told me that Victoria wasn't his." He paused, waiting for my reaction.

"You mean she was adopted?" I supplied, pretending this was news to me. The old guy relished telling a dramatic story, and I didn't want to disappoint him.

"That's the thing: she *wasn't* adopted, not formally. Joan and Ted had been trying for children for years without success. Then a friend of Ted's—well, I don't think they were friends, they'd gone to high school together or something, but they moved in different circles—this man got a girl pregnant. He was well-to-do, and the girl—an Irish lass—was his children's nanny. Catholic, so she wouldn't agree to an abortion. It was all hushed up. The girl was shipped back to Ireland and gave birth in one of those Magdalene laundries run by the nuns—you've seen the film."

I hadn't, but I knew what he meant. Unmarried Irish girls who got pregnant were put to work in the laundry and their babies taken away to be adopted by good Catholic families.

"The baby was Victoria? But how did she end up back in Philadelphia with the Hartmans?"

"The father—this rich man—had a change of heart, found religion or something. Anyway, he felt guilty, and wanted to give his child a good start with a family he knew and trusted, so he wangled it with the nuns—probably gave them a wad of cash—and brought the baby back to America. He gave her to Ted and Joan, no questions asked or answered, no paperwork, no formalities, nothing! They registered her birth here in Philadelphia as if she was their own newborn. Ted told me he also gave them a house in Manayunk. It wasn't much in those days—we're talking thirty-five years ago—but it was a big step up from the rental the Hartmans were living in. Now, with the increase in house prices, and Manayunk being one of the most desirable suburbs, the place just sold for over two million."

Two million dollars: the major part of Victoria's inheritance. "Did Ted tell you this rich guy's name?" I asked.

"No, but he said the whole story was in the letter that I was to give to Victoria after he died." Another letter to be opened after death. That's where Victoria got the idea for her letter to Gaston. Anderson continued, "I urged Ted to tell Victoria all this in person, but he wouldn't. I didn't understand why until Victoria came to me in September to draft her own will."

I nodded to myself. I understood too. Ted Hartman

couldn't face telling Victoria that she was adopted when she had given up her own baby for adoption, perhaps pressured to do so by her father. He'd taken the coward's way out, writing it down, knowing he wouldn't have to see her anger or disappointment when she read it. But why had Victoria written to her son, with similar instructions to the lawyer? It didn't make sense. Surely, having been deceived about her own origins throughout her life, Victoria would be eager to find her son and forge a connection with him. I needed time to think this through, but Anderson was still speaking.

"How did Victoria get those drugs she took? Was she prescribed them by her doctor?"

My mouth fell open as I realized I had never asked this basic question. Where *had* the drugs come from? Some detective I was! I had neglected the most elementary steps in the investigation. Not only the means of death, but also the scene—I should have arranged for the doorway recess where she was found to be taped off and processed by a CSI. I should have recorded follow-up interviews with the couple who found her, not rely on the statements they gave to the uniformed officers who were first on the scene, and I should have had those officers canvas the street for other witnesses. Instead, when I sauntered in to work the morning after the body was found, I had read their report and filed it. The body had already been transported to the morgue, but it wouldn't have been too late to process the scene. I'd never thought of it. I guess I'd just assumed another homeless person kicked the bucket. Police work makes you callous that way.

Instead of starting with Victoria's death, I'd plunged into her life. Eager to get to know the *real* Victoria and explore her background, I had rushed across the country to Philadelphia. I'd only attended the autopsy in the first place because I was intrigued by the ruggedly handsome Dr. John Williams, Medical Examiner, and look how that had ended up. A proper detective would have initiated inquiries with the airlines and local hotels to discover how Victoria came here, where she stayed, and who was the last person to speak to her. I would have to start all over again, two months late.

"I don't know," I said, answering Anderson's question. "But I'll find out. And I'll find Gaston Lemesur, Victoria's son."

"Good. I have to go. Keep in touch, won't you?"

He finished the conversation leaving me feeling depressed. In spite of the commitment I'd just made to Anderson to continue the investigation, it felt like a daunting task. I hadn't asked Anderson any of the questions I'd prepared: about Victoria's letter to her son, what she had said about her future plans, her state of mind. I sat there mentally kicking myself until the sun came up and I realized I had only half an hour to get to work.

****

Once in the office, I began to formulate a plan to fill in the gaps in the official record. Using the joint drug task force investigation as a cover, I made a data retrieval request for all files on all drug overdose deaths in the last three months. I knew this would produce Victoria's autopsy report which I had already reviewed. This time, I'd concentrate on the specific drugs listed as present in her body. Then I'd find out from Dr. Luchinski whether any were prescriptions he'd written for her. I'd have to think some more about my approach with Luchinski. I didn't want him complaining to John that I was demonstrating obsessive-compulsive tendencies again.

I could also employ the drugs investigation to justify a canvas of local hotels. Hotels are often drug trafficking sites: anonymous, lots of comings and goings. Of course, I'd bury Victoria's name amongst the list of other drug deaths when I asked if these individuals had taken a room. I should also go back to the street where Victoria was found and see if any business owner had noticed anything unusual on the evening she was found. Just visiting the scene might give me more ideas.

Chapter 12

That evening, I started a new murder wall. This one was a timeline. Instead of using flimsy little sticky notes, I plunged in with a black marker. At the far right of the eye-level line I drew across the bare white wall of my study, I wrote "October 13—9 p.m.—body found" and made a mark. Under the mark, I wrote "430 Front Street." A little to the left, I indicated the range of time within which Victoria had died: six to nine p.m. Then I stood back to survey my work. I didn't think the landlord would appreciate it, but I could paint it over before—if—I ever moved.

On my way home from work earlier, I had visited Front Street, and loitered opposite number 430 for a while to get a sense of the scene. This was a short, quiet road on the edge of downtown, not much traffic. The buildings were fifty or more years old, small apartment blocks and offices, none taller than three stories. Of the two shops, one was empty with a "For Lease" sign in the window. While I watched, five people left number 430: office employees on their way home, I guessed. When the building was in darkness and ten minutes had passed without any activity, I crossed to the entrance. Double glass doors were set back about four feet from the sidewalk. Nameplates on the side wall of the recess announced that an Allstate insurance agency occupied the ground floor, and a business called Trans-Pacific

Logistics was on the second. The third floor was vacant. To gain entry, visitors had to press a buzzer and speak into an entry phone. A keypad on the door allowed workers to let themselves in with a code. I peered through the doors into a dim lobby. The place was asleep for the night.

I walked over to the shop on the corner, a dry cleaner. The sign on the door said the store closed at six. I was just in time.

"Hi, I'm with the police department, following up on the discovery of a body across the street back in October." Remembering Jerome Pinter's complaint, I didn't flash my police badge or hand the man behind the counter my business card.

The storekeeper was a trusting soul and didn't ask for ID. "Yeah, I heard about that. I'm gone soon after six, so I didn't see anything myself. Can't help you." Trusting, but eager to close the store and hurry home to his dinner.

"How did you hear about it?" I asked.

"Mickey told me about it." The man pointed above his head. "He rents the apartment upstairs. Never misses a thing that goes on in the street. Poor old guy—doesn't get out much."

"You think he'll be home now?"

"Sure to be."

Glad to get me out of his hair, he directed me down the side of the building to the back where metal stairs led up to a door at the second-floor level. I knocked and waited. After a long minute, I heard shuffling steps and the door opened. Mickey was probably in his seventies, with straggly gray hair and watery pale eyes. His clothes were clean though, and his tentative hello sounded more curious than hostile.

I repeated that I was following up on the discovery of the body in October. "What do you remember about that night?"

"Well, the police car and the ambulance—all the flashing lights. But then they turned them off, and I knew she had to be dead. They don't stop traffic for a corpse."

"You saw that it was a woman?"

"Yes, I can see right into the doorway over there. I can show you." Mickey led me down a short corridor into a room that combined kitchen, living and dining. The window that gave onto the street was curtained against the winter night. "I saw them bending over her, a couple of passersby, and then the ambulance and the police. I didn't have the curtains closed back then. I like to enjoy the light as long as it lasts." I got the impression the old man was lonely, and welcomed a visitor, even a cop.

I stepped over and pulled the drapes aside. He did indeed have a clear view across the street to number 430. Even on a dark December night, the doorway recess was visible. It would have been dark too at nine o'clock on October 13 when Victoria's body was discovered, but no doubt the lights of the emergency vehicles illuminated the street.

"What about earlier that evening when it was still daylight? Did you see anyone in that doorway, say, after six?"

He shook his head. I pressed him a little. "It would still have been quite light until nearly seven o'clock, right?"

He shrugged. "Of course, I'm not sitting looking out the window all the time. Six o'clock's my dinner time.

I'd be fixing some food, eating it, clearing up." With a wave of his hand, Mickey indicated the small kitchen area, and the table and two chairs in a corner. "Mind you, I do like to watch the sunset, and so I sometimes take my dinner and sit by the window while I eat. I can't tell you whether I did that evening or not—depends whether there was a nice sunset."

"If you had been looking out of the window between six and seven, would you have seen someone in that doorway?" Yes, I was leading the witness, and his statement of what he *hadn't* seen was hardly evidence, but I was becoming convinced that Victoria had not died in that doorway but had been placed there after dark. Although the street was quiet, I didn't believe a conservatively dressed, clean-looking person would have lain there in daylight for up to three hours without attracting notice.

"I probably would have seen someone if they'd been there, yes. Not much happens on this street that I don't see. I keep an eye out for the homeless. They don't usually come up this way, but if I do see one, I usually take out a warm drink or a piece of cardboard for them to lie on. There but for the grace of God…"

"Thank you, Mickey." No further questions.

****

So where had Victoria died? I stared at my timeline, unable to add anything until I answered that question. I remembered the autopsy report stated that, when discovered, Victoria showed no *rigor mortis* or lividity—the gravitational pooling of blood to the lowest point in the body. Rigor and lividity don't show up until about two hours after death, so there was nothing to say Victoria *hadn't* died in that doorway as late as seven o'clock, except the likelihood that Mickey would have noticed her there.

I heated up a can of soup and ate it with some stale crackers. I was out of wine, so I finished a random bottle of vodka that had been hiding behind the individual pizzas in the freezer compartment. Nicely anesthetized, I fell into bed.

Victoria came to me again—not a nightmare this time. She was sitting on a bed in what looked like a hotel room, and dressed in one of those white terrycloth robes that hotels provide. At first, I thought maybe it was me sitting there. Then the figure looked up and smiled in my direction, not at me but at someone behind me. I turned and saw a young man in the doorway, his face in shadow: Gaston. I tried to say his name, but couldn't get the word out. Victoria was still smiling.

When I woke, I knew with absolute certainty that Victoria had come to this town to meet her son. I don't know where that conviction came from unless Victoria was somehow communicating with me through my dreams. I was intrigued by the idea. I'd always dismissed those charlatans who called themselves "forensic psychics" and turned up whenever a child went missing. *"I sense she's somewhere dark, perhaps below ground?"* And then, when the body turns up in a shallow grave or hidden in a basement, the clairvoyant's photo is in the paper with the headline, *"If Only They'd Listened to Me."* But they hadn't the same relationship to those victims that I had with Victoria; we were doppelgängers, for Christ's sake. Shared DNA wasn't the only indicator of connection. Whether or not Victoria was speaking to me from the beyond, my belief that Victoria's journey west was to reunite with Gaston, and that her death was a consequence of that meeting made it all the more urgent to trace her movements in the hours and days before she died.

****

I couldn't wait to get back to the office the next day when I should have the response to my data retrieval request. I'd have to at least skim all the files retrieved in order to put something convincing in the joint task force database, but I'd concentrate on the contents of Victoria's file—the police report and witness statements.

There were thirteen drug overdose deaths in the three-month period I had specified. I sorted through them, not meaning to linger but finding them strangely compelling. The detective instinct, I suppose, driving me to question the assumptions made by my fellow officers and the M.E.: "homeless," "heroin addict," "history of mental health issues." I pulled out eight that had fentanyl listed amongst the drugs in the deceased's system—something to note in the database because fentanyl was the drug we were following—and then I turned to Victoria's file.

The police report, with its stilted language and reliance on incident codes, added nothing to my understanding of the crime scene. The patrol car had turned up after the ambulance, and the officers had relied on the paramedics for the statement that Victoria was dead when they arrived, making efforts to revive her unnecessary. There were no photos of the scene, the police officers noting that the paramedics had already moved the body out of the doorway to facilitate their preliminary examination and search for identification.

The witness statements from Annette and Carlton Minter were more interesting. Their interviews were recorded and transcribed. They were returning to their parked car, after dining in a restaurant a couple of blocks away, when they found the body.

"I noticed her shoes first," Annette Minter stated. "I have a pair just like them. I knew they cost more than a hundred dollars, and hers looked almost new. I said to my husband, 'She's not homeless. We should help her.' Carlton tried to wake her by shaking her arm."

"She was sitting folded over, her back towards the corner of the doorway and her feet towards the sidewalk," Carlton said. "I lifted her shoulders and when I saw her face, I realized she was probably already dead, but I felt for a pulse in her neck, and to see if she was breathing. Then I called 911."

Carlton asked the 911 dispatcher for an ambulance, and, as an afterthought, for the police. The ambulance arrived eight minutes later. "While we were waiting"—Annette took up the story—"I noticed her clothes: nice black pants and a knitted jacket with toggle buttons. The buttons were done up wrong, as if she'd dressed in a hurry. When the ambulance people arrived, they undid the buttons, so they could listen for a heartbeat, I suppose."

Besides confirming that they had seen no one else hanging around on the street before finding the body, and giving their contact details, the witnesses had nothing more to add. I made a note of their phone numbers but didn't think I'd contact them. Their detailed first impressions gave me plenty of food for thought, and I doubted whether two months later they could add anything useful. "Folded over"—to fit into the trunk of a car? Buttons done up wrong "as if she'd dressed in a hurry"—or as if *someone else* had dressed her!

I *had* to find out where Victoria was staying before her death. As I wracked my brain for a pretext to do a hotel canvas with Victoria's photograph, I flicked through the eight fentanyl-related folders. The deceased were a diverse collection: a Latina hotel maid, a male community college student, and a forty-year-old nurse stood out from the usual suspects who were long-time substance abusers with histories of petty crime. One of the latter group had died in a notorious motel known as a hangout for dealers. Another had listed the same motel as his mailing address. That was a start, but I didn't think Victoria had been a guest there. Then I noticed an unusual coincidence: the hotel maid worked at a hotel out by the airport; the nurse who lived in Denver and was supposed to be visiting family in the area was registered as a guest at the same hotel. The place was a respectable lodging for business travelers and tourists—far from being a druggies' lair. In fact, it was just the kind of place where Victoria might stay after flying in from the east coast.

I quickly assembled a list of hotels in the area, making sure to include the three near the airport. I pulled up photographs of some suspects in the fentanyl smuggling ring, and added mug shots of felons I knew were serving long stretches behind bars. I created two "six packs," photo arrays with two rows of three photos in each, and inserted Victoria's picture in the lower row of the second one. I was thinking of what I should enter into the joint task force database as justification for the canvas before setting out, when a voice hailed me from the other side of the squad room.

"Hey, McQuarry! When are you coming down to Evidence to look at those seven boxes I pulled for you?"

I looked up. Big Eddy supervised the secure evidence room in the basement. He'd been shot in the knee by a fleeing felon years before, and his pronounced limp rendered him unfit for regular patrol duty. For a moment, I couldn't think what he meant. Then I realized that my data retrieval request had included *everything*—physical evidence as well as reports and statements. It felt like everyone in the room was looking at me, as I floundered. I had no intention of wading through the putrid drug paraphernalia and filthy clothing these boxes contained, but I knew Big Eddy wouldn't let it go until I gave him an answer.

"Yeah, yeah. I'll be down later today. I've gotta…um. Later, okay?"

Myers, Kleinberg's pet, broke the silence that enveloped the room. "You onto something, McQuarry? Come on, share it! We're all on the same team here." He gave me a false smile, all teeth, knowing I had never been on his team, or anyone else's for that matter. Everything I had achieved as a detective had been on my own and in spite of my so-called colleagues. They were all waiting for my response, waiting for me to stumble. I had to think fast.

"It's just a hunch I'm checking out. Don't want to jinx it. Might be nothing…"

"Hmm," Myers nodded knowingly. "Just a hunch, eh?" As the rest of the squad room resumed their background chatter, he dropped his voice and leaned towards me. "Well, I've got a hunch that you're headed for trouble. Be careful; the captain's got his eye on you." He sounded concerned, but I wasn't taken in. Myers wanted my sergeant's spot. I tried to look impassive, but inside I was shaking with a mixture of fear and rage. I *had to* solve Victoria's murder, even if it put my job at risk. But my job was all I had. I snatched up the folder with my list of hotels and the photo arrays and left without meeting Myers' eye.

As I walked to the car, I remembered I hadn't entered anything in the database recording my intended activities. I considered going back and concocting something about the fentanyl overdoses, the airport hotel connection, tying it all together with a theory about drugs coming in through the airport. But I couldn't face Myers again. I imagined all my colleagues turning to stare at me, the token woman, "not a team player," off chasing her hunch while they slogged away at routine tasks. I'd log in later. Who knew? Maybe I'd have something to back up that theory.

Chapter 13

James Anderson, the attorney handling Victoria's estate, reached me by phone as I left the first hotel on my list, the seedy motel and druggie hangout associated with two of the fentanyl OD deaths. The rain was pouring down, and I was still seething from my recent encounter with the paunchy, malodorous manager.

"Can you hold on until I get to my car? It's raining here." I liked Anderson but his communication style was long-winded; I needed shelter and a moment to switch gears before I could listen.

The motel manager had taken his time emerging from a back room when I approached the check-in desk. No doubt watching kiddie porn, I thought. He barely glanced at the photo arrays I showed him, after explaining who I was and what we were investigating.

"Nah, people got privacy rights. I not help you," he said in a heavy Eastern European accent. "You come back with warrant—"

"If I come back, it'll be to close this shithole down!" I snarled. Oops, there goes the Department's commitment to collaborative community policing. If he made a complaint, I'd be in trouble, but, what the hell, I was in trouble anyway, and this joker in a grease-stained sweatshirt made my blood boil.

Sitting behind the wheel, watching rivulets of water descend the windshield, I resumed the call with

Anderson.

"I think you might be interested in the fruits of some research I've been doing," he began. He embarked on a circuitous explanation of how, typically, it is the responsibility of the buyer of real estate to conduct a title search to ensure that ownership can be transferred free of any lien on the property. However, as Victoria's estate was still in probate, he, as executor, had initiated a title search of Ted Hartman's house in order to speed up a sale.

"You will recall that Victoria's biological father gifted the house to Ted and Joan when they took the baby, so—"

I snapped to attention. "You've discovered the identity of Victoria's father! Who is it?"

Anderson seemed a little miffed at being interrupted. "Nathaniel Ditton," he responded slowly. "He was a well-known Philadelphia philanthropist from a Mainline family. He died several years ago."

"The Ditton Foundation," I stated.

"Yes, indeed. He established the foundation to benefit local children."

"And Victoria donated about $180,000 to it before she left town in October."

Anderson hadn't known that. "Oh, I wonder why. I'm sure she was unaware of her real father's name."

I supplied more information. "And Stein Pinter, Victoria's employer, represents the foundation. I thought maybe she heard about the foundation at work, but when I was in Philly I met with Andrea Faber, the director of the charity. There's something fishy going on there. She wouldn't tell me anything, but when I mentioned Gaston Lemesur, she certainly reacted. I wonder if the Ditton

Foundation had anything to do with placing Victoria's baby back in 2002. After all, her parents already had a personal connection with Nathaniel Ditton through Victoria's placement with them when she was a baby. They knew they could rely on his discretion."

"That's certainly a possibility," Anderson mused. "Anyway, how are you getting along? Have you found out whether the drugs that caused Victoria's death were prescribed to her?"

Damn! I'd forgotten all about calling Dr. Luchinski. I hadn't even looked at the autopsy report for the specific drugs she OD'ed on. Maybe I'd unconsciously avoided the task. If I made further inquiries about Victoria to Luchinski, there was a strong chance the doctor would contact his pal and fellow doctor John Williams, who already thought I was unbalanced. John would relish passing on his confirmed assessment of my mental state to my bosses, telling himself he was only concerned for my wellbeing, but happy to get back at me for spurning his advances.

Anderson was waiting for a response.

"I'm concentrating on Victoria's last hours. I think she died elsewhere and her body was dumped in the doorway where it was found. I also think she met Gaston here before she died." I didn't add that my "evidence" for the latter conclusion was a dream.

"Okay. You carry on with that aspect, and I'll interview this Andrea Faber. I might get Jerome to help, as he represents the foundation, and is also trying to find Gaston Lemesur. Let's keep in touch."

We terminated the conversation, and I set off towards the airport. The hotel connected to two of the fentanyl deaths was next on my list.

The lone clerk on duty at Reception studied all the photos with care. However, he did not single out either the Latina housekeeping employee or the Denver-based nurse. Perhaps he had no contact with the below-stairs staff and had not checked in the nurse who had permanently checked out on drugs in one of the guest rooms. But it was that quiet, middle-of-the-day period when the lobby was empty and the employee was happy to chat.

The clerk looked up with a grin. "You're kidding, right?"

"What do you mean?" I asked.

"You're trying to trick me—that's you!" He laid a forefinger on Victoria's head shot, randomly arranged between two other women, one a Canadian suspected of drug trafficking, the other a local who'd succumbed to her addiction a month before Victoria died.

"N—no!" I stuttered, shaken. I turned the array around and stared at the photo. Perhaps, with my hair plastered to my head with rain, and my complexion washed out by weeks of not eating or sleeping properly, I did look like Victoria's corpse. I shook my head to rid my brain of the image. "So, you don't recognize any of these other people?"

"No, but I'm one of three that work the desk, and we see hundreds of people every week. It's hardly surprising."

I thanked him and left. Was I on a fool's errand? Why would a hotel employee remember a guest from two months ago? I considered abandoning the canvas. I couldn't face another receptionist identifying me as a dead woman. It would feel like a dire prediction—the cold hand of fate resting on my shoulder.

The next hotel on my list was just down the road. I'd give myself one last chance to discover where Victoria had stayed before her death. Again, there was only one person on the desk—a young woman this time. Her name tag identified her as Danica. She welcomed me with a smile, and I explained my mission.

She looked at each photo in turn, biting her lower lip in concentration. When she finished, she went back to the first array. "This man has stayed here a couple of times recently. I can't remember his name, but I know he's Canadian." She had identified one of the RCMP's big fish suspects, Larry Cremond. I gave an internal whoop of elation: now I had something to contribute to the database. Then she turned to another sheet of photos. "And I think I recognize this woman."

My heart gave a leap: Victoria! How to play this? I needed confirmation, but my brain kept replaying the seedy motel manager's warning: come back with a warrant. I'd never be able to get a warrant. "Why do you remember her? You must see hundreds of guests."

Danica laughed. "I've only been in the job eight weeks. I remember all my first guests because I'm learning the process. I'm still in training but I'm much quicker now. If you have a name for this woman, I can confirm her stay from our records."

God bless the trainee! She didn't know I had no right to ask her to check the guest register without a warrant. I knew I was wrong to take advantage of her innocence, but I had already strayed so far I couldn't stop now. "Victoria Hartman. She was probably here in mid-October."

With a few key-strokes—I could see she was proud of her new skills—Danica had a result. "Here we are:

Ms. Hartman reserved two rooms for three nights, checking in on October 11. She checked out early, though, on the thirteenth."

I was buzzing with excitement. "Who had the other room?"

Danica studied the screen. "Hmm, that's odd. We're supposed to get an ID for the primary occupant in each room, but there's no name listed for the second room." She frowned. "Unless…"

"Unless what?" I prompted

"Unless the room is occupied by the minor child of the primary guest," she finished in a rush, evidently quoting from memorized Standard Operating Procedures. Gaston! The second guest had to be Gaston!

"How did she pay? Credit card? Cash?"

I was pushing my luck and Danica was becoming uncomfortable. "I don't think we're supposed to give out that information. Anyway, I wasn't on duty when she checked out. It was in the evening. She would have had to pay for the third night…"

I needed to leave before she called her manager. "That's fine. Thank you so much for your help, Danica." I flashed her a big grin and a just-between-us-girls wink.

I held off from doing a victory dance until I reached the car. Victoria had stayed at this hotel—*with Gaston*. She had checked out—or someone else had checked out for her—on the thirteenth, even though she clearly planned to stay until the fourteenth. It was inconceivable now that her death was suicide or accidental overdose. If only I had police privileges to examine border crossings, tracing Gaston through his passport would be a cinch. He was potentially the key witness to his mother's murder, and perhaps to her killer.

Although tempted to ditch work and hurry back home to fill in the new information on my murder wall, the time was not yet three o'clock and it would be wiser to return to the office and report to the database. The squad room seemed strangely quiet when I arrived. Half the desks were empty, but Myers was still there, hunched over his computer, head down, not acknowledging my presence. I strolled past him, confident in the knowledge that I could now back up the hunch I'd claimed earlier.

When I reached my cubicle, I pulled up short in shock. Seated at my place, head thrust forward toward the computer screen, sat the captain, his normal unhealthy flush darkening to an angry puce.

Chapter 14

"My office. Now"

As I followed Captain Kleinberg, my mind raced with possibilities. Had I failed to log off from my computer when I rushed out earlier? I thought I had, but wasn't sure. What might have been on my screen? Had the captain seen Victoria's file on my desk along with the other files of recent ODs? Or the notes I had scribbled on scraps of paper as I prepared the photo arrays? Was there anything incriminating in them? It also occurred to me that the seedy motel manager might have phoned in a complaint about my aggressive behavior. Unlikely, but I decided to keep quiet until I found out which of my sins had found me out.

Kleinberg sat down and fixed me with a baleful glare. Left standing, I resisted the desire to shuffle my feet and tried to keep my face expressionless.

He started slowly, in a more-in-sorrow-than-in-anger tone. "We're a team here—a family." I suppressed a nervous giggle. *Not my family.* "I've got four officers committed to this fentanyl inquiry. Three of them are working hard: reviewing CCTV tape, checking border crossing records, doing surveillance on known drug offenders." He paused before beginning again in a louder voice. The door to his office was open—deliberately, I presumed, so the whole squad room could listen to my dressing-down. "And then there's you! Never share, never report in. Going AWOL on the basis of some hunch!"

I felt a surge of relief. My ongoing investigation into Victoria's death, pursued against the captain's specific orders, was safe. As soon as I'd left the building, that jerk Myers must have whined about me not sharing information. Kleinberg might harass and insult me, but he wouldn't dare fire me, the only woman on the squad, and risk a discrimination lawsuit. I could handle this.

I opened my mouth to defend myself, but he raised the volume still further. "What about the chain of command do you *not* understand? What about inter-agency cooperation? You're supposed to log your activities into the joint task force database *before* you go wandering off the reservation to pursue some hunch." He coated the word "hunch" with sarcasm.

"Permission to speak, sir?" I inserted the request as he took a breath. "The hunch paid off. Larry Cremond, identified by the RCMP as a B.C. drug cartel boss, has made at least two recent visits to our neighborhood." I rapidly explained that I had pulled the files of seven recent fentanyl-caused deaths and linked two to an airport hotel. "It occurred to me that although they use low-level mules to get the drugs over the border, they'd have to send a boss down on occasion to check on the operation, sort out personnel problems, that kind of thing—a quick in-and-out through the airport. I put together some head shots and got lucky at a hotel near the airport. I should have entered this into the database before I left. I apologize. It won't happen again."

The captain's eyes bulged as he digested my report. I could see the internal conflict play out over his features. He wanted to continue reaming me out, but he had to acknowledge the value of the information I'd presented. His glare still fixed on me, he yelled, "Myers!"

Myers must have been lurking outside, because he arrived lickety-split, attempting to look innocent but coming off as stupid.

"Larry Cremond." Kleinberg was addressing Myers, not me. "I want you to liaise with the Canadians. Get a full background—rap sheet, known associates—everything you can. Then get with Customs and Border Control: all crossings in the last six months. Check airport entries first. Then work up a warrant application for registration records at this airport hotel. It seems Cremond is a frequent guest. While you're at it, include CCTV in the warrant. They have cameras in the lobby. We might catch who he meets with."

Myers had pulled out a notebook and was making furious notes. He'd be a busy boy.

"I could help with the hotel registration records and CCTV review," I volunteered, thinking how I might catch Victoria and Gaston on the video.

"No," the captain replied curtly, and continued talking to Myers. "You got all that? Keep in close coordination with the other agencies, and report back to me twice daily." He waved Myers away. As the young detective left, he grinned at me. I shot him a look calculated to curdle his blood, but he'd already turned his back.

"You, McQuarry, will do a deep dive on the recent fentanyl ODs—full details on the deceased, their friends, family, employment, education, health records—everything." This was busy work and he knew it. It would chain me to my desk for days. "But before that, you need to update the database: share the fruits of your private investigation with your colleagues—better late than never. But before *that*—" he was shouting again— "Clean up your damn desk! It's a disgrace: scraps of paper, dirty coffee cups, files all over the place! A tidy desktop shows an ordered mind."

How dare he treat me like a fifth grader? I struggled to find a suitable retort, then realized it was pointless: Captain Kleinberg's mind—like his desktop—was a blank expanse, unable to comprehend the nuances of my investigative method. I pulled my shoulders back, nodded, and walked out of his office.

I spent the rest of the afternoon crafting a lengthy report to the database, replete with unnecessary detail such as weather conditions (Fahrenheit *and* Centigrade temperature readings for our Canadian readers) and geographic coordinates. Childish? Yes, but I was in a weird mood, on the one hand, elated by discovering Victoria and Gaston's hideaway. The fresh start she had planned back in Philadelphia had become a reality, if only for a brief moment. On the other, the knowledge that I was all alone in this fight to find out the truth about her death depressed me. I was not just alone. My so-called "family" of colleagues was actively working against me, impugning my motives, my methods, even my mental state. Well, except for James Anderson, but he was a continent away and hardly the warrior for justice I needed at my side anyway.

On the way home from work, I picked up a couple of bottles of wine and a frozen chicken pot pie. I put the pie in the oven and took one of the bottles to my spare room. I had information to fill in on the timeline. A while later, going back to the kitchen for the other bottle, I discovered I had failed to turn the oven on. Oh, well, never mind. I fell asleep on the sofa soon after.

****

When I arrived at work the next morning, Big Eddy was talking to the uniform on the front desk.

"Hey, McQuarry! What about that evidence I pulled for you?" His gravelly bellow across the lobby attracted the attention of a handful of citizens waiting to file their sundry complaints. They looked from Big Eddy to me, then back at him, anticipating some kind of drama.

"Yeah, I'm on it. I'll check in and then be right down." I gave him a wide smile, disappointing the onlookers. After all, I had been ordered to complete a work-up of the fentanyl deaths, and an examination of the sordid remains assembled in the evidence boxes in the basement was as good a place to start as any.

I peeled a pair of thin latex gloves from the box on Big Eddy's desk, and put them on. Eddy said nothing but indicated with a jerk of his head a row of bankers' boxes lined up on a table against the wall of the evidence room.

The first box I opened pertained to the Latina hotel housekeeper. I'd learned from her skimpy file that Marta Gutierrez was a Guatemalan immigrant who had applied for asylum after crossing the border to El Paso three years ago. She was a single mother with a teenage son and a younger daughter, no criminal history, and had been employed at the hotel for two years. She also worked for a home cleaning service. Her body had been found in her car parked at the far edge of a parking lot. I thought she was an unlikely drug user, but who knew.

Her work uniform lay folded over the rest of her effects. The smock was a pale blue synthetic, with her name tag pinned to the front. I could see the outline of a piece of card through the thin material of the breast pocket. I pulled it out. "431 LC." Was this a license plate number? Or maybe a room number—a cleaning assignment? I took a photo of the card with my phone to ponder later, and continued my search. The rest of her box, and the next several contained nothing much of interest, except a couple of cheap phones—probably burners—that I bagged and labeled to send to the techs for analysis of phone records. This should have been done as soon as the bodies were found, but before our department joined the fentanyl task force, drug-related deaths were barely given any attention. "They got what they deserved" seemed to be the usual police reaction.

Although my data request a few days earlier had sought the files on all overdose deaths in the last three months, physical evidence would only be retained for those deaths connected to criminal activity, for example, illegal fentanyl use. The personal effects of those who died from an overdose due to legitimately-obtained prescription drugs would have been returned to their next of kin. Eight fentanyl ODs turned up as a result of my data search, so I was a little puzzled to see a ninth box. I opened it without even looking at the label on the side, and was confronted by a knitted cardigan jacket that I immediately recognized—Victoria's!

I reeled back in shock. I had been unprepared to see her belongings, the clothes that had last touched her body when she was alive, when she had been reunited with her son, when she had faced her killer. Before I could stop myself, I leaned forward and delved my hands under the pile of clothes, lifting them up and burying my face in them. A faint scent—fresh, floral—still clung to the wool. Victoria's hugs would have smelled like this. I was crying, my tears soaking into the fabric, releasing yet more of the fragrance, and a deep well of grief I hadn't known existed. Grief for Victoria—her life cut short just as she had found her son and started a new chapter; grief for myself—my isolation, my hopeless quest, my miserable life.

After a minute, I got a grip on my emotions, aware of Eddy behind me. Had he noticed my shoulders slumped over the evidence box, heard my sobs muffled in Victoria's clothing? Then the realization struck me that any DNA evidence of Victoria's killer on her jacket was now irretrievably tainted. I wanted to scream in frustration. Instead I refolded the clothes carefully, replaced the lid on the box, and scooped up the evidence bags containing the phones. Eddy was still engrossed in his crossword puzzle.

"You want to log these?" I indicated the bagged phones. "I'm taking them for further analysis."

Sighing, as if performing the basics of his job was a gross imposition on his time, Eddy took down the details without looking up at my ravaged face.

"The boxes can be reshelved now, thanks," I said and left.

Chapter 15

John appreciated how Coalport did Christmas. No snow, but scarves of white mist wreathed the Douglas firs and created shimmering halos around the ubiquitous strings of colored lights. Familiar Christmas music swelled into the street whenever a shop or café door opened. Even the crowds, swaddled in their puffy jackets and woolen hats, seemed like characters out of Dickens, all rosy cheeks and ready smiles—much more authentic than the adobe, palm trees, and seventy-eight-degree heat he was used to at this time of year.

Although Perry and Ed had lived here a shorter time than John, they had already gathered a wide circle of friends. They were planning a big celebration on Christmas Day, and John was invited over after hosting them on Thanksgiving.

"You were so sweet to put up with Britney—she's back in rehab now, by the way, so we can really cut loose," Perry said. "Bring that gorgeous Christine. Might be good to have a police presence in case the party gets totally out of hand."

"Uh, yeah…I don't think she'll be able to make it, but I'll be there. What can I bring?"

"Just the pleasure of your company!"

John was determined to find the right gift—something extravagant and unusual—to repay their generosity. He'd covered most of the downtown shops and galleries, and couldn't decide between an antique table lamp that he was almost sure was Tiffany and a Pendleton blanket in a stunning black-and-white Navajo design. Perry and Ed could display it as a wall hanging or use it on a bed. John thought maybe he should buy a present for Christine too. He knew there was no point. She wanted nothing to do with him. After he'd cooled down, he'd tried phoning her, but the call went straight to voicemail. He didn't leave a message. What could he say? Apologize? For what? For caring about her and trying to protect her from herself?

He couldn't stop thinking about her though, wondering what she was doing for Christmas, whether she had any time off. She'd said she had no family, but that might just have been one of her sweeping doom-laden declarations. Everyone had some family. John had a brother in California. He and Nancy went there for Christmas two years ago. It was awful—teenagers on their phones, brother and wife squabbling, too much food and way too much booze. Perhaps Christine would go back east for the holidays, in which case John hoped she steered clear of Luchinski and any of Victoria's other contacts.

John knew he should get back to work but instead found himself parked across the street from the police department. He wasn't going in. He would just sit and watch for ten minutes in case she came out. Then he'd decide whether to get out of the car and speak to her. Ten minutes became twenty... thirty. He was cold. It had started raining again.

It was early afternoon when Christine emerged. She looked terrible—gaunt, hunched over, her hair greasy and unkempt. John couldn't believe the change in her in just a couple of weeks. Perhaps she was undercover on some drug bust, but if that were the case she wouldn't be walking out the front entrance of the police station in broad daylight. He was so shocked he gave up any thought of approaching her. She crossed the road and passed right in front of his car without recognizing it. She seemed in a stupor, eyes fixed on the ground in front of her. He watched her walk until she was out of sight, his hands gripping the wheel, his breathing ragged.

What should he do? If he pursued her and tried to talk to her, they'd likely get into an argument, her accusing John of being patronizing and controlling. She was so determined to be independent. But the need for an intervention was clear. She was in crisis and she might try to harm herself. John could never forgive himself if that happened and he had done nothing. He looked back at the police station. Captain Kleinberg was probably at his desk. Christine had no respect for him, but maybe she misjudged him. Anyway, it was the captain's duty to take action to protect the health and welfare of one of his subordinates.

John locked the car and headed across the road to the police department entrance, thinking about how he could introduce the subject of his concerns. He had an excuse for his visit—to update the captain on the increasing number of fentanyl-caused deaths he was seeing at the M.E.'s office. Fentanyl mixed with heroin, ketamine, and other drugs, young people experimenting, as well as older hardened drug abusers.

Kleinberg was available. After John had run through his informal report, he asked how the task force enquiries were going, and whether they had identified the source of the drug.

"We know it's coming from British Columbia," Kleinberg said. "We have yet to identify how it's coming across the border, but we will. A matter of good old-fashioned police work, chasing down every lead, surveillance, cross-checking records. Boring work, most of it."

John saw his opening. "That must put a tremendous strain on your officers."

"Oh, most of them understand what's needed and just get on with it. Teamwork, good communications, persistence, that's what gets results. Of course, there's always one who thinks they can solve it on their own." Kleinberg gave a huff of disgust.

"Christine McQuarry?" John ventured.

The captain's eyebrows shot up. "You know her?"

"Yes, quite well. And to be frank, I'm a little concerned about her. Her dedication to the job is admirable, but we all need balance in our lives—"

"You think she's unbalanced?" the captain shot back.

"No! Well, I mean, I see signs of stress. Sometimes, it seems she's almost obsessed. That can't be good for her in the long run."

"Hmm," the captain leaned back in his chair and nodded several times. John thought that was encouraging. Christine's boss appeared to understand his unease. He'd just leave it there.

Standing up, he asked Kleinberg about his holiday plans, voiced some platitudes about the weather, then left.

Chapter 16

I couldn't stay in the precinct any longer. I had to get out. I didn't want to go home to the grubby apartment, the empty refrigerator, the gaps on my murder wall. So I just walked, head down, shaking hands stuffed in pockets, head aching, and mind on replay: Kleinberg's hectoring voice, Eddy's indifference, the smell of Victoria's clothes. I lost track of time and place.

As it got dark, I became aware I had wandered to the waterfront—the ugly industrial stretch lined with shuttered warehouses and vacant lots. I stepped over the collapsed chain-link fence surrounding the ruins of a factory that had burned down years before. Anything salvageable had been plundered, leaving smoke-blackened brick walls with gaping spaces where doors and windows had been. It suited my mood. I walked through the detritus left by those who had used this shell to conceal their activities: drugs and illicit sex. Tattered blankets and broken shopping carts indicated a refuge for the homeless too. If Victoria's body had been dumped here instead of on a well-lit street, the rats would have discovered her first.

I emerged from the other side of the building onto a bluff. A low wall separated me from a steep drop to the water. The tide was high. The seawater looked black and oily, absorbing light rather than reflecting it. I wondered—not for the first time—what it would feel like to sink through those inky depths, to relax into the darkness. Would my body react instinctively, lungs burning, arms flailing, fighting upwards even as my mind sought oblivion? I had a surer, quicker way to end it: I'd left my service weapon locked in the bottom right-hand drawer of my desk in the squad room. Messier perhaps, but I wouldn't be the one to clean up afterwards.

Shaking my head to clear the bloody image, I took a step back from the edge. I needed to concentrate on finding my way back to my car. I picked a path through the ruins to return to the road. My thoughts—if not lighter—were at least more focused. I needed a drink.

The first bar I came to looked rundown, with grimy windows and a sputtering neon sign advertising beer. Perfect. I wasn't looking for craft ale and ambience. I entered. Early evening and the place was crowded, men in clothes that suggested they worked in the area: construction boots and donkey jackets. A few turned to stare at me, not used to seeing a lone woman come in who wasn't on the game. I walked up to the bar, thinking of what I could order that would have the quickest effect.

The barman was engaged in conversation with some other customers and refused to catch my eye. After a few minutes I called out, "Hey." He slid his eyes over me, said something I couldn't hear to his buddies, then approached, wiping the counter down with a towel as he came.

"Double vodka, hold the rocks," I said.

"Do you have a preference for brand?" The heavy sarcasm with which the bartender spoke alerted me to the fact they only had the one kind—a cheap no-name—so I just shrugged in response. I downed the drink in two swallows, then waited for the heat to hit my stomach and the glow to move up to my brain. It was taking too long.

"Same again."

He refilled my glass without comment. Then retreated up the bar to resume his conversation. I turned and looked around the place, confirming my first impression that this was a working men's bar, and I wasn't welcome. An older man glared at me while a couple of younger guys grinned unpleasantly. I didn't frequent bars, preferring to do my drinking at home on my own. This place validated my preference. I finished my vodka and paid up.

The bar was on the corner of a narrow street, more of an alley. I stopped to get my bearings, the cold night air making my head swim after the fug of the bar. I glanced back into the alley and noticed a couple. The man was heavyset with long greasy hair and a leather biker jacket. He had his hands against the wall on either side of the woman's head. I couldn't see her face but she looked to be half the size of her boyfriend. He was berating her, growling words I couldn't make out. She was cowering, trying to make herself even smaller. Suddenly he grabbed her around the throat with one hand, lifting her off her feet.

"Hey! Hold on!" I was on my way across the street when he tossed the woman aside and turned on me.

"What's it to you, bitch?" He came towards me, arms held out from his body, ready to strike. I heard the skitter of footsteps as the woman took her chance to escape.

I put a hand in my pocket to find my police badge, but before I could get my fingers on it, he swung at me. Alcohol must have slowed my reactions because, although I ducked to the side, he still landed a heavy blow on my collarbone. Training kicked in, and I went in low, attempting to use his size and clumsiness against him. I punched him hard in his considerable gut and followed up with a kick aimed at his groin. I missed and lost my balance for a moment, long enough for him to swing again, connecting with my temple. I crumpled to the ground, my last thought as I slipped into unconsciousness was the mugging outside the Philadelphia bar. Why was this always happening to me?

I opened my eyes an unknown time later to see four uniformed legs. Painfully, I lifted my gaze. Two patrol cops were standing over me. I didn't recognize them, but they knew me.

"Sergeant McQuarry? What happened?"

Well, this was embarrassing. The street was empty now, no frightened girl, no greasy thug in a leather jacket, not even a curious customer from the bar. I briefed them in as few words as possible.

"We got a call—a woman, wouldn't give a name. Lucky we were close." The younger of the two patrolmen helped me up. The way he tilted his head away told me he'd smelled the alcohol. So much for vodka being undetectable on the breath.

The older cop took over. "We'll have to write this up, but honestly, in this neighborhood, no one's going to give us information. Just another crime statistic unless you can ID the assailant."

I shook my head. "Nope, never saw him before, and I didn't even get a glance at the woman. If you could just give me a ride to my car—"

"Sorry, ma'am. Can't let you drive in this condition. We need to get you to the ER to be checked out."

"No!" That would turn embarrassment into

humiliation: they'd do a blood-alcohol test. "I feel fine. Look, how about we compromise? I won't drive—you can take me to my door. I promise I'll see a doctor tomorrow if I need to."

"Who's going to monitor you tonight, Sarge? Concussions are tricky," the older guy seemed genuinely concerned.

"My roommate's an EMT," I lied. "She'll take care of me."

They sat me in the back seat of the patrol car. I heard the automatic door locks click and smelled the pine disinfectant with underlying notes of vomit and piss. I'd never ridden in the back seat of a police car before, and I didn't relish the experience. Better than an ambulance, I guess. I leaned back and closed my eyes. My head was throbbing. I didn't think my collarbone was broken, but I knew I'd have some colorful bruises the next day. The buzz from the vodka was long gone. I felt nauseous and shivery. If only I'd been quicker to draw out my badge and yell "Police!" I might have forestalled the attack. Or if I hadn't been disoriented by the alcohol, I could have handled the big guy, no problem. Hindsight was no help, so I needed to shift into damage control mode.

Forcing myself to open my eyes and lean forward, I spoke through the narrow gap in the plexiglass screen that separated me from the front seat.

"Hey, guys, before you call in to Dispatch, could we have a word?"

The younger cop was driving, and only spared me a quick glance in the rearview mirror. The other one turned around in his seat. "Okay, what's up?"

"You've heard about the joint drug task force, right?" He nodded. "So I'm assigned to follow up on some fentanyl overdose deaths." I took a breath. This was where I would step away from the truth. "I'm undercover, following a lead about a dealer in that bar back there. Look, I screwed up—I shouldn't have reacted to that brute beating up on his girlfriend, breaking my cover like that. Should have walked on by—I acted on instinct, you know? But it'll totally wreck my investigation if you report my name over the radio. You know all the geeks and weirdos in town are listening in on the police frequency. Someone could pick it up and work out what I was doing. Can you just leave me out of it? Say you arrived at the scene and found no one?"

The older cop stared at me. Was that pity in his eyes? He sighed. "You know I can't do that. I can keep your name out of the over-the-air report tonight, but it'll be in the written incident report. Nothing I can do 'bout that."

The other one snorted and shook his head. His disdain was aimed at me, not his partner, who was unhooking the handset on the radio.

I fell back again, staring out the window in a daze, hearing the drone of the officer's words as he called in the incident, explaining that they were transporting "the victim" to her residence. In a few hours, when the cops ended their shift, my name would be in a public and searchable police record as a person involved in a brawl outside a bar.

Perhaps I should have accepted that watery invitation to jump after all.

Chapter 17

After John left Captain Kleinberg, he went back to his office. He had reports to finish writing, but couldn't settle down to it. He felt a creeping dread that he had done the wrong thing in sharing his concerns with Christine's boss, that he'd made things worse instead of better.

Kleinberg had listened without comment, except to nod occasionally, which John had taken to be understanding and empathy. Now, he remembered a strange gleam in the detective's eyes, as if he were relishing John's confidences. John had qualified everything he said with phrases like "I might be mistaken" or "perhaps this is just the normal stress of the job," but had he gotten Christine into trouble?

John gave up on the reports and went back to the shop with the Navajo blanket. While the salesperson was gift-wrapping it, he wandered around the store, picking up things randomly to examine them. A beautiful but simple statue attracted his attention: a female figure, feet together, arms by her side, only the suggestion of features on the face, about eighteen inches high.

"Lovely, isn't it?" The proprietor had come to stand next to him. "It's a copy of a piece in the Athens Archeological Museum from the Cycladic era." He saw John's bewildered look. "Twenty-five hundred years BCE. More ancient than Ancient Greece."

"She stands like a soldier. Did that culture have female warriors?" John asked, thinking of the Amazons.

"I don't think so. More likely she's a virgin being readied for sacrifice to the gods."

He decided to buy the statue for Christine. Whatever the man said about human sacrifice, to his mind the figure showed defiance and strength. She was Christine. He hesitated when he saw the price tag: $320. Then he chided himself. He'd have spent that much on Nancy, and he had the money.

"I'll take it. Can you gift wrap that too?"

John felt pleased with himself. The sick feeling in his stomach that followed the interview with Captain Kleinberg receded. He'd take the present to her apartment right away. He wouldn't stay or get into a discussion, just give it to her, wish her a Merry Christmas, and leave. She would at least know that someone cared about her, saw her as brave and worthy. It might be enough to change her mood, lift the despair that seemed to weigh her down.

He parked opposite Christine's apartment building. Before opening the rear door to retrieve the wrapped box containing the statue, he peered up at her floor: no lights, she wasn't home yet. It was nearly seven p.m. She wouldn't be long. He got back in the car to wait.

As the minutes ticked by, John began to worry. Earlier in the afternoon, his first thought had been that she might harm herself. The thought returned and grew into near panic. Should he go search for her? Return to the police department and clarify his earlier vaguely expressed concerns in order to get the uniformed cops to look out for her? He argued with himself that he was overreacting, she'd turn up in the next five minutes. He'd wait.

He was checking the dashboard clock for the umpteenth time when a police car pulled up outside the apartments. The driver opened his door and the interior light came on. John could see Christine sitting in the back. He watched in bafflement as Christine climbed out. She stumbled, and the cop who had been driving grabbed her arm, supporting her as she tottered towards the building. She was drunk. John felt a confusing mix of emotions—relief that she was okay and she hadn't killed herself, along with disgust and anger at her inebriated state. Once she had entered the code for the entrance doors—it had taken a couple of attempts—the patrol car moved off.

There was no way John could face her at this moment. He needed to take time to sort out his feelings. She needed time to sober up.

Chapter 18

When I woke the next morning the temptation to pull the covers over my head and slip back into unconsciousness was overwhelming. Every bone in my body ached and my head throbbed like someone was banging on it with a hammer. After a few minutes, I staggered to the bathroom. Only after I saw my face in the mirror did I realize that one eye was swollen shut. Ugly red and purple bruises spread out from eye socket to hairline. I'd swallowed a handful of ibuprofen the night before but fallen into bed without icing the place where the goon's fist had landed. Although it was probably too late to make much difference, I wrapped an icepack in a towel and retreated to my bedroom to lie down again.

I had to go in to work. The captain had given me an assignment—deep background on the fentanyl deaths—and his beady eyes were fixed on me. My absence might give him the ammunition he wanted to make my life even more miserable. Then I remembered that the incident report from last night would have been filed by now. How long would news take to reach Kleinberg? I had to get there first to try to ward off the consequences with some bullshit explanation. But what?

A long hot shower helped. I towel-dried my hair and found some clean clothes. Digging deep into a drawer in the vanity, I unearthed some foundation I hadn't used in months, maybe years. I don't wear makeup unless you count lip salve, but I used the foundation to cover up the bruising, then pulled locks of my still-damp hair forward. It would have to do.

A strange silence thickened the air in the squad room when I entered. Every head was bent forward, no one making eye contact except the captain who stood in the open doorway to his office. I guess the uniform on the front desk had called up to warn of my arrival. Kleinberg jerked his head, indicating I should follow him into his office.

"Shut the door. Sit down." This was new. Only two days before, he'd kept me standing while he shouted his displeasure loud enough for the whole floor to hear. I sat, and he did too, looking down at his clasped hands in front of him.

"It has come to my notice that you have been showing signs of stress. Others have observed this too, including a medical professional." He sounded as if he was reading from a script, using formal language quite unlike his usual rants. However, the script was not the document on which his hands rested, a lone page placed in the center of his desk. Now that I was seated opposite him, I could see that this was an incident report—*the* incident report. What was he talking about—stress? Why wasn't he screaming at me about unprofessional conduct?

"And so I have decided to place you on medical leave, effective immediately."

What? I stared at him in disbelief. I hadn't requested sick leave. I didn't *want* sick leave. Then, in a flash of understanding, I saw it: this was how he'd get rid of me with no blowback. He'd come off as the compassionate boss, caring for the health and well-being of his officers, and I couldn't complain of harassment, discrimination or unfair treatment.

I was speechless with shock for a moment before I gasped out, "How long?"

"Indefinite. You will need to pass a fitness-for-duty examination before you can resume your duties."

I could pass a fit-for-duty exam that afternoon, no problem. I was pretty sure he had no intention of allowing me to try. In a stronger voice, I demanded again, "How long?"

He pursed his lips and frowned at the ceiling as if consulting an invisible calendar stuck up there. "We-ell, let me see. I'll probably schedule you for an interview with the police health officer in…February. Provided of course you make suitable progress in the interim."

Two months! I'd never been away from the job for more than a week. How could I survive two months? Being a detective was my life. I'd fought and clawed my way into the job, and now he was snatching it away. The injustice took my breath away.

"You will receive full pay while on leave," Kleinberg said. "I'll need your badge and your weapon." He stood up to indicate the meeting was over. He still hadn't looked me in the eye.

I sat motionless, cemented to the chair, my hands gripping the arms. I glared at him, shooting lasers of venom from my eyes. He didn't care. He tapped the incident report twice with his forefinger, a final unspoken message, then went to open the door. I wanted to scream. Instead, I rose slowly with as much dignity as I could muster and left his office.

The background murmur in the squad room fell

away; heads drooped over desks. I had made my way over to my cubicle before I realized Captain Kleinberg was following me. When I sat down, he stood next to me, hand outstretched.

"Now! McQuarry." He wanted the badge and gun. I retrieved the badge from my jacket pocket, and unlocked the drawer that contained my service weapon in its shoulder holster. I placed both items on the desk. Kleinberg picked them up.

"You'd better clear out any personal items. We'll need the space for another detective." There was no pretense I would return to work. He turned and walked back to his office.

After a minute, the buzz of chatter resumed. I pulled out my backpack from under the desk and started assembling the few things that belonged to me: a box of tissues, some snacks. I noticed the files at the left of the desktop: the eight fentanyl OD cases I was supposed to research. Victoria's file was in that stack too. I wanted desperately to have it. After all, no one else was interested in a closed file, a suicide. But I knew if I started sorting through the files to find Victoria's, I might attract attention. The whole stack was only a couple of inches thick, no more than half a dozen pages in each folder. My pulse quickened as I laid the backpack on the desk, its unzipped mouth next to the files. I glanced up. No one was looking in my direction. I slid the whole pile into my pack, then stuffed a sweater on top. At a more leisurely pace, I went through the rest of the drawers for any other personal belongings. I zipped up the backpack, shouldered it, and walked out without saying goodbye.

I managed to hold it together until I reached my car, parked where I'd left it more than twenty-four hours ago—in another lifetime, when I had a job and a purpose. I folded my arms over the steering wheel, laid my head on them and let the tears flow, taking great gulps of grief, shoulders heaving. A glance in the rearview mirror told me tears, snot, and dissolving makeup were making channels down my face onto my neck. The rain overnight had beaded the windshield and windows, veiling my meltdown from passersby. I'm not sure what I would have done if some well-meaning soul had stopped to inquire whether I was all right…snarled and screamed, frightening them away, I guess.

At last, I cried myself to a standstill. I felt drained, exhausted, numb. Wiping my face on my sleeve, I started the car and headed for home.

Chapter 19

As I entered the apartment, I realized I had not seen the place in broad daylight for days. The low winter sun slanting through the windows lit up the dust motes and glinted off the plates piled in the sink. The trash can was overflowing and a sour smell permeated every corner. I went to the bedroom to hang up my jacket, thinking about curling up for a nap, but the sheets hadn't been changed for weeks. I stared at the unmade bed, the glass on the nightstand stained with red wine dregs. I was disgusted with myself. I'd been living like a slob—how had I gone downhill so fast? Only a few weeks ago, I'd been rocking along, solving cases, staying out of the captain's way, keeping myself fit and the apartment clean. Now I teetered on the edge of an abyss. Without a job, I could see myself tumbling down into a chaos of alcohol and bitterness. Things had to change.

I started by dragging the sheets off the bed and shoving them into the washing machine. I retrieved the dirty glass and the empty bottle rolling around under the bed, and took them to the kitchen. I attacked the mess there with manic energy, washing dishes, wiping countertops, mopping the floor—twice, until my feet no longer stuck to it. Next, I confronted the bathroom. Two hours later, hot and sweaty, I downed a big glass of water and surveyed my domain. It was, at least superficially, spotless. God knows what alien life forms persisted inside the oven and the fridge, and there were at least two more loads of dirty clothes stashed in the bottom of the closet, but they could wait until tomorrow. There was satisfaction in bringing a surface-level kind of order to my life, and I hadn't thought about the job once—well, maybe once. Or twice. I had avoided opening the door to the office. I was unprepared to confront the incomplete timeline and the murder wall with all its unanswered questions.

Right now I was thinking how hungry I felt. I hadn't had a meal since early the previous day. I rifled the cupboards, knowing the fridge would offer nothing edible beyond an array of condiments: chili sauce and horseradish relish didn't appeal to me. I found a can of tomato soup and a packet of crackers. The crackers were stale but submerged in the soup they tasted okay. As I spooned them up, I opened my phone to the Notes app and started a shopping list. Real food: fruit and vegetables, cheese and eggs, orange juice and milk. I would cook, I would clean, I would start running again, and read Jane Austen and *Moby Dick*. I'd learn to play chess or pickleball or both. I would *not* play the defeated victim, the role assigned by Captain Kleinberg and my colleagues. I flashed on Kleinberg's reference to "a medical professional" who had concurred in his stress diagnosis. Who could that be? Of course! John Fucking Williams, Medical Examiner *extraordinaire*, male chauvinist control freak and know-it-all! I experienced a moment of blinding rage before taking several deep breaths. John would *not* destroy my resolve to make a fresh start. I would not allow him that power over me.

I finished my meal and washed the bowl. Glancing around, my eye rested on the backpack I'd dropped inside the door when I came in. I thought about the files inside. What impulse had driven me to take them? I already knew the paltry contents of Victoria's file by heart. The other folders—the fentanyl overdose deaths—were a random bunch with nothing in common except that little or no police investigation had been carried out on them. But they each represented a life and a life story; they merited more. I decided I'd take a look, spending no more than an hour before I put them aside and set out to do my grocery shopping.

I fanned out the folders on the table, considering where to start. The one that intrigued me was Marta Gutierrez, the Guatemalan hotel maid. Why had she struggled to escape with her two children from the gangs and violence of her native land, undertake what must have been a hazardous journey to the United States, and then succumb to drugs? She had held down a regular job at the airport hotel for more than two years, apparently a good employee who volunteered for extra shifts. She had no history of drug or other offenses. And yet on October 3, ten days before Victoria's death, she had been found in her parked car in a hotel lot, dead from an injection of heroin laced with fentanyl.

The autopsy report was brief: no underlying disease, no obvious signs of struggle, a single injection site on the inside of the right elbow. There were some minor cuts and abrasions on her hands, but these were consistent with the kind of manual work she performed daily. Under the illegible signature, I read the typed name "John S. Williams, Medical Examiner."

Other details were sparse. She left a sixteen-year-old son, Frank, and an eleven-year-old daughter Gloria. Her address was on the north side of town in an area of small apartment buildings that immigrants could afford.

I remembered the piece of card in Marta's uniform pocket, and opened the photo I had taken on my phone: "431 LC." The significance of these letters and numbers still escaped me, but because she had them with her at the time of her death, I suspected they might be important. There were no phone records in the file. Either the investigating officer hadn't thought pulling the records was necessary, or—less likely—Marta had no phone. There hadn't been one in the evidence box I had examined yesterday, which might mean it had been returned to her next-of-kin along with other personal items like keys and wallet.

I decided to visit Marta's children, but it was only 2:30 p.m., the kids wouldn't be home from school yet. Then I remembered this was the day before Christmas Eve: school winter break. I'd do the grocery shopping on the way home.

The address led me to a shabby duplex with a bare front yard. The door was opened by a heavily built man in his forties.

"Hello. I'm looking for Frank Gutierrez. Is he here?" I smiled, trying to look as non-threatening as possible, but the man glared at me without speaking.

I tried again. "It's about his mother's death. I just wanted to clear up a few things. It won't take long."

He turned away, and I feared he was about to shut the door in my face. I debated whether to insert my foot in the gap, but I no longer had the authority of the police department behind me, so aggressive tactics would be a mistake. He didn't close the door. Instead, he spoke over his shoulder in rapid Spanish to someone I couldn't see. After a few seconds, a girl of seventeen or eighteen replaced the man. Similar build and facial features declared her to be his daughter or niece. I stated my purpose again.

"They don't live here anymore," she said in accented English.

"Do you know where Frank lives now?" I asked.

"Why?" She was suspicious. I knew why: the Latino community had much to fear from unknown visitors. And I remembered the colorful bruises that marked my face. Maybe I didn't present as so nonthreatening.

"Look, I'm not from Immigration or the police or anything. I'm investigating his mother's death. There are some details I'd like to clear up—"

"Who are you? The police didn't think it was worth investigating. Why are you interested?" Good question. Why *was* I interested?

"It's difficult to explain. Soon after Frank's mother passed, a woman I know died of a drug overdose too. I think she might have been murdered. I wondered whether there might be a link between the deaths. The woman I know was staying at an airport hotel—"

The girl interrupted again. "Where his mom worked?"

"No, another one." As I spoke the words, things started to fall into place. Previously, I had barely registered the fact that Marta Gutierrez had been found dead in a parking lot, *not* at the hotel where she worked, but at the other airport hotel where Victoria had been a guest. The hotels were close, about a quarter of a mile apart on the same wide avenue leading to the terminals, but why had Marta left her place of work and gone to another hotel? As I brought the two hotels to mind, another revelation occurred to me: Marta's place of employment was a two-story structure; Victoria's hotel rose up at least five floors. If the number on that card in Marta's pocket was a room cleaning assignment, it was for a room on the fourth floor. That could not be part of her job but it might be a room at the other hotel.

While I pondered, the girl was assessing me. "Wait here," she said, and closed the door, leaving me on the step. She had remarkable self-confidence for a teenager and seemed smart. If she decided to trust me, I thought she'd be an important ally.

She came back dressed in a hoodie. "I'll show you." She set off without waiting for a response from me.

I hurried after her up the street. "I'm Christine. What's your name?"

"Teresa." She tossed the word over her shoulder.

"You know Frank, then?" I accelerated to keep up, wondering how far from my car she was leading me. I began to feel nervous.

"We both go to Lincoln High."

I wanted to ask more questions, but Teresa pulled out a phone and started talking into it in Spanish. After about fifty yards, she turned into a cul-de-sac lined with low apartment buildings. A few kids kicked a soccer ball around, and a couple of men standing over the open hood of a car stared at us.

"So, you're taking me to Frank's place?"

She had finished her phone call. "Yeah, he'll talk to you, but you'd better be straight with him. He doesn't need any more hassle."

She led me up an exterior staircase to a long balcony onto which apartment doors opened.

"Frank and Gloria live with cousins now." She stopped at a door and entered without knocking, pulling it shut behind her so I was left on the balcony feeling exposed. A minute later, Teresa returned accompanied by a good-looking youth with the beginnings of a beard. He wore a hoodie like Teresa's, shoulders hunched, hands in pockets.

"Frank? Is there somewhere we can talk?" I didn't mind Teresa sticking around, but I'd hoped for a private space.

"Here's good." Frank's accent was pronounced. He affected the self-conscious defiance of a teenage youth, but I saw he was edgy. He swept his eyes over the street below and along the balcony before meeting my gaze. "What you wan'?"

"I want to find out why your mother died. I think she might have been murdered."

"You police?"

"No. I used to be. This is…personal."

Teresa had taken up a watch position leaning over the balcony rail. Without turning, she said something in Spanish.

"Your frien' murdered also?" Frank asked.

It seemed too complicated to explain that Victoria wasn't my friend, so I just nodded.

"Drugs?"

I nodded again. Frank pushed his hands deeper into his pockets and frowned. I waited.

"In Guatemala, gangs everywhere, drugs everywhere. They make young kids—seven, eight years—to work drugs. My mama say no—her sons, no. Then my little brother—" He broke off, bringing his chin up and squeezing his eyes shut for a moment. "She bring me and my sister to America to escape drugs. She keep us safe. Then they come again."

"Guatemalan gangs? Here?"

"No! Not Guatemalan! White guys, nice cars. At school, at basketball games, after football practice. Mama say no—her son, no! Tha's why they kill her."

I turned to Teresa. "Have I got this right? Drug dealers are recruiting at the high schools? Frank's mom confronted them?" Teresa nodded. The fentanyl task force hadn't uncovered any of this. I couldn't see any connection to Victoria's death other than the airport hotel. "Have you told the school? Don't you have a school security officer? What about the police?"

Frank made a dismissive sound, and Teresa laughed. "They wouldn't believe us. Look at how they treated Marta, calling her a druggie, saying she OD-ed."

"Could you identify them? The ones dealing drugs?"

Frank and Teresa exchanged a look. Frank grimaced and took a step back toward the apartment door.

"Wait!" I urged. Frank shook his head and disappeared inside, shutting the door.

"Identify them? Then what?" Teresa sneered. "You're not police. You can't keep him safe. Even if you was police, you couldn't protect him. He has his sister to look after. His mother's dead, and no one cares." She pushed past me and headed for the stairwell, me tagging along behind, trying to find words to reassure her but realizing they would be false.

Marta Gutierrez's death had been too easy to write off as a self-administered drug overdose, just like Victoria's. The police—and the Medical Examiner—had failed them both. I was reluctant to admit the fact, but I was implicated in that failure too. If I hadn't been so intent on proving myself the smartest cop in the department, disregarding procedures and alienating my coworkers, perhaps I'd have had a chance to put things right. Now, excluded from inside information and evidence-gathering tools, it might be impossible.

Chapter 20

John had finished the autopsy and was in the prep room peeling off protective gear when his admin assistant signaled from the doorway that he had a call.

"Take a message and say I'll call back in ten." He needed a few minutes to gather himself. The autopsy had been upsetting: a sixteen-year-old boy, high school basketball star and only child. John would have to wait for the forensic test results to come back, but he was pretty sure it was a fentanyl overdose—fentanyl mixed with some painkiller in a kitchen pill factory, then pushed to kids with an assurance that it was the best high they'd ever have. His mother had found the boy's body when she went to his room to rouse him for breakfast. *Some Christmas those parents will have*, he thought.

When he returned to his office, he was surprised to see that the phone call had come from Dr. Luchinski. He considered ignoring it, remembering his last exchange with the Philadelphia doctor and what it had led to, but professional courtesy overcame this impulse.

"Thanks for calling back, John. This is about Victoria Hartman—you remember, my patient who was found dead in Coalport?"

John winced inwardly. Victoria's death had brought nothing but confusion into his life.

"I've received some information that I wanted to pass on. I tried to reach Detective McQuarry, but they told me she's no longer with the police department, so I called you."

"What?" John stiffened, but Luchinski continued, oblivious. "I had a visit from a lawyer, James Anderson. He's the executor for Victoria's estate. He's represented her and her family for years, apparently. He asked me whether I had prescribed the medications that she overdosed on."

John was still trying to process what Luchinski had said about Christine no longer being with the police department. He must have misunderstood or misheard. Christmas Eve—only a skeleton staff at the department answering calls—maybe Christine had already left on holiday leave.

"I'm sorry, you were saying the lawyer asked about the overdose? I think he has a copy of the autopsy report."

"Yes, he does. He wanted to know whether these were drugs I prescribed for her. They were not." Luchinski sounded hesitant, even embarrassed.

"Maybe another doctor—" John suggested.

"No, I'm certain Victoria would not have gone to another doctor for them. She was so careful, even about over-the-counter medications. She worried about harmful interactions with the treatment she was on." Luchinski paused, seeming to invite John to comment, but he couldn't yet see where this was leading. "Anderson doesn't think she killed herself. He thinks she was murdered."

That's what Christine thinks too. Now John understood Luchinski's unease, and he began to share it. When they had spoken last, both doctors had agreed suicide was the likely cause of death, and that Christine's theory that Victoria had been killed by someone else was outlandish. Maybe they'd got it wrong.

"There's something else Anderson said," Luchinski went on. "Victoria had a son. He was given up for adoption as a newborn, but she was determined to find him. There's nothing in her medical records about pregnancy or childbirth, and she said nothing to me when we discussed her medical history. I'd been feeling guilty about missing signs of depression or suicidal tendencies, but now I feel bad that I jumped to conclusions about her death without all the information."

You feel bad, John thought, *but you weren't the one who signed the autopsy report.*

"I'm not sure what I can do. The body's been cremated. I'll pass this on to Chri—the police here and put them in touch with Anderson. Can you give me his number?"

"Oh, they already have it. Well, I won't take any more of your time. Happy Holidays!" Luchinski disconnected, leaving John staring at the phone in his hand, thinking back to the autopsy he had conducted on Victoria Hartman's body. Had he missed something?

Since he'd taken this job less than a year ago, most of the autopsies performed on unexplained deaths had turned out to be drug overdoses of one kind or another. New in the M.E. role, he'd relied on the police, often not even going to the scene of death if, as in Victoria's case, the cops had already made the judgment that there was no reason to suspect foul play. He had plenty of excuses, the primary one being that the M.E. position had been vacant for some weeks before he took over and there was a backlog to clear. The office was underfunded and short-staffed. He had already drafted a budget proposal for the coming year to add an assistant medical examiner and upgrade the laboratory equipment. But perhaps he should revise the protocols left by his predecessor; even if TV crime dramas, with their teams of crime scene investigators accessing instant DNA results, were unrealistic, improvements could be made.

As he recited these justifications to himself, John was uncomfortable. Christine hovered at the edge of his thoughts. He should go see her. Two nights ago, he'd assumed she was drunk. He was learning not to make assumptions. Perhaps she was off work sick. Perhaps he could help her, look after her. The office was closing early today. As soon as he had written up his notes from this morning's autopsy, he would go to her apartment. The gift-wrapped box containing the statuette was still on the back seat of his car.

Chapter 21

I went for a run in the morning. After a mile, I was winded and had to slow to a walk. Baby steps.

Back at the apartment, I took a shower. I was pleased to see the bruising around my eye had faded to blue-gray from the purple-red of the day before. I'd had a decent night's sleep and my head didn't throb anymore.

Scrambled eggs and toast for a late breakfast. I could open my refrigerator without dread, having cleaned it thoroughly before stocking it with the fruits—*and* vegetables—of my grocery shopping last evening. Now I needed a plan to steer me through the day. Clean the oven? Do the rest of my laundry? That wouldn't even take me to lunchtime. The tightrope I was walking required minute-to-minute concentration. I was afraid if I had too much spare time to think about my predicament I'd spiral down again.

The files were still spread out on my table. I decided to continue my review, interspersed with housekeeping: one file, one cleaning task, an attempt at a balanced life. When I sat down with a second cup of coffee, the Marta Gutierrez file pulled me in again. My visit to Frank yesterday had provoked questions that needed follow-up. I drew a notepad toward me and started a list.

"White guys in nice cars" hanging around the high schools, for example. How could I alert the drug task force to this? I knew I couldn't just stroll into the police department. I could make an anonymous report on the tip line. Maybe this wasn't urgent, as schools weren't in session right now.

Marta's phone? I'd meant to ask Frank about that, but he'd cut the interview short before I had a chance. I should go back and try again. But would he talk to me? Remembering it was Christmas Eve gave me an idea— I'd take Frank and Gloria Christmas presents. What do teenage boys want—besides teenage girls? I had no idea. Or what an eleven-year-old girl might like, either. I'd been that age once, but could not conjure up a single memory of opening a gift. I'd go shopping later and maybe inspiration would come.

I also needed to call James Anderson. I had shirked the task of finding out whether Dr. Luchinski had prescribed the drugs found in Victoria's system, but I had other information to share with him now. I knew where Victoria had been staying in Coalport before her death, and I was pretty certain she had met up with Gaston. I'd have to admit to the attorney that I'd lost the trail. Explaining I was "on indefinite leave" from my job would not be pleasant. But maybe he'd learned enough from the Ditton Foundation to reopen the inquiry into Victoria's death from his end and I could still play a role.

A rush of elation at this thought spurred me to search for Anderson's number. After five rings, a recorded message came on in Anderson's pleasant, rather formal tones: "The law offices of James Anderson and Associates are closed for the Holidays until December 28th." Elation turned to anger. I clenched my jaw, imagining Anderson in an ugly Christmas sweater surrounded by cherubic grandchildren and ho-ho-ho-ing in front of a roaring fire. Offices closed until after the holiday? How dare he abandon the case like that?

I was pacing the living room, trying to think of how to get Anderson's home number when the buzz of the entry phone surprised me. I so rarely have visitors, I had to think for a moment to identify the noise. I unhooked the handset on the unit next to my front door. "Yes?"

"Christine, it's John. Can I come up?"

My immediate reaction was *Hell, no! Go away, you little shit!* But I said nothing, breathing deeply to master my rage, and trying to think rationally. What was he doing here? What did he want?

"Christine? Are you there? I need to speak to you." He sounded unsure of himself.

"Well, I'm listening," I said. I was not in a mood to cut him any slack.

"Not like this. I mean face to face. Please let me in. I want to apologize."

This was a surprise, the great John Williams saying "sorry." Curiosity induced me to press the button to unlock the entry door. While waiting, I cast a glance around the apartment, pleased that it was clean and tidy. I shouldn't care, but I was also sneakily glad I'd showered and dressed in a decent sweater and fresh jeans. What was wrong with me? I was finished with the M.E. after what he'd done.

I spotted the files on the table, scooped them up and looked for a place to stow them out of sight. I wasn't supposed to have them, and John's penchant for ratting on me was established. Opening the door to my office/second bedroom, I flung the files on the bed. Sparing a quick look at the walls with their notations in black marker, I shut the door behind me just as John knocked.

He held a gift-wrapped box under one arm, and a grocery bag showing grease stains in the other hand. "Hi, Christine—God! What happened to your face?"

"It collided with a fist a couple of days ago," I replied, deadpan. I stood six feet away, arms crossed. "What's this apology you mentioned?"

He pulled a face, halfway between a smile and a grimace. "Yes, I brought a peace offering—Philly cheesesteaks, your favorite?" He extended the bag towards me. I didn't take it, although the aroma was making me salivate. "They're better warm," he urged.

I shrugged, turned to fetch two plates and a roll of paper towel. We sat at the table. I busied myself with unwrapping the sandwich, not speaking. He had placed the box on the floor against the wall. I assumed the gift was for me but I wasn't going to comment. I hadn't thought of buying him anything. In fact, I hadn't bothered to buy a single Christmas present and hadn't expected to receive any. Stupid waste of money in my opinion. Still, I wondered what it was.

John seemed to be fumbling for a way to start. "I had a call from Dr. Luchinski this morning."

"Oh?"

"Hmm. He now has doubts about whether Victoria committed suicide."

I nodded as if disinterested, my mouth full of cheesesteak.

"He told me he didn't prescribe the drugs she OD'ed on, and he doesn't think she got them from another doctor."

"And...?"

John took a big inhale. "And...he said he'd tried to call you but was told you're no longer with the department."

I nodded again. In a flat voice, I said, "I'm on indefinite medical leave for stress. Based on your diagnosis, I believe."

"No! I never—I just wanted…" Was he going to cry? Of course not. He pulled himself together. "I made a mistake going to Kleinberg. I should have spoken to you, not him. I was worried about you. You looked so distressed."

"Really? When was this? Were you stalking me, John?" My voice rose to a screech. I shouldn't have let him come up. All the progress I'd made—making healthy choices, leveling out my life, the deep breathing—all out the window.

"I wanted to see you. I care about you. I hate the way we parted on Thanksgiving." He spoke in a ponderous tone. Like Kleinberg the day before, he didn't meet my eye.

With difficulty, I calmed myself. I concentrated on finishing the cheesesteak, chewing slowly, relishing the flavor. I thought about my plan for the afternoon, returning again to the problem of what to buy for Frank and Gloria.

My eyes must have wandered to the gift by the wall, because John broke the silence. "I hope you like what I bought you. It reminded me of you: your strength against the odds."

What could I say, except, "Thank you. Should I open it now?"

"I was hoping you would." John smiled for the first time, and I felt a flash of what had attracted me to him at the beginning.

I peeled off the paper and opened a sturdy box.

Inside, muffled in more wrapping, was a pale stone statue, about eighteen inches high, a female form, feet together, hands at sides.

I gasped, "It's beautiful!" I didn't understand what John had said about the statue reminding him of me. The girl was young and thin, with barely any breasts, the suggestion of hollows for eyes and a bump for a nose, her shoulders were hunched a little, her feet seemed out-of-proportion large. In its entirety, it was stunning, ageless, poignant beyond words.

John pointed to a leaflet in the bottom of the box. "That tells you about the original this is copied from, the history and theories about the culture."

Right then, I couldn't care less about history and culture. I turned to John. "Thank you. This is…too much. I don't have anything for you."

"I don't want anything. If you like it, then that's enough for me."

"I do like it." I placed the statue on the table between us.

John wiped his mouth on a piece of paper towel and got to his feet, awkward again. "Listen, if you're not doing anything tomorrow, how 'bout coming with me to Perry and Ed's place? They're having some people over for Christmas dinner—you don't have to bring anything."

"I…um, I'm not sure," I stammered, still moved by the beauty of the statue. "I'm not really fit for company at the moment."

"But it's Christmas! You can't be alone at Christmas!"

I didn't want to go into the countless Christmases I had survived quite well thank you in the company of take-out food, books and videos. And wine. "I'll be fine."

"I'll call you tomorrow. Maybe you'll change your mind."

Please go before you spoil the moment by being overbearing, I thought. *I want to be alone with my girl.*

He took the unspoken hint, and left.

I needed a minute to get myself back on track. Wondering why the statue spoke to me with such intensity, I sat staring at it. Then I made the connection: although vertical rather than horizontal, the figure's posture was identical to how I had seen Victoria's body lying in the morgue—feet together, hands by her side, face without expression. John said the girl reminded him of me, determined against all odds. But that wasn't me. It was Victoria. She was the resolute one, unwavering in her search for her son and planning a new life together. I would call my new possession Victoria—not out loud, of course. I wouldn't want John to think I was crazy!

Laughing at that thought, I got to my feet. Victoria couldn't stay perched in the middle of my dining table. She needed a better platform to project her forthright character. I unplugged the television set I never watched and moved it from the credenza into my bedroom. I'd never watch it there either, but the relocation left an appropriate surface clear for Victoria. She looked magnificent against the slate blue wall I had painted in a short-lived fit of home decorating after I first moved in.

Satisfied, I retrieved the OD files from the office-bedroom and spread them on the table again, repositioning my chair so that I could look up and exchange affirming vibes with my girl. Now I could concentrate on my list of questions for Frank.

Chapter 22

Darkness had fallen before I made it to Frank and Gloria's apartment. I'd spent a fruitless half hour wandering the aisles at the largest discount department store in Coalport, trying to find suitable gifts. I didn't know the kids' clothing sizes, or what sports and games they liked. In the end I bought them each a hundred-dollar gift card. Their needs might be more basic than video games. Teresa told me that cousins had taken them in after Marta's death. I imagined stretching finances to cover two extra mouths to feed might be challenging; the gift cards would help.

No children kicking a soccer ball around this time, or men standing over an open car hood, but decorative lights shone from several uncurtained windows. However, when I climbed up to the second floor, I found no lights on in the apartment where the Gutierrez children lived. I knocked and waited, knocked again. A woman came out of the next apartment and said something fast in Spanish—perhaps informing me the neighbors were out. I nodded, said "*Gracias*," and descended to my car.

I panicked that the kids had moved on again—maybe back to Guatemala? The thought was ridiculous—Frank had been here only the day before. I was overreacting; nowadays any minor frustration tended to throw me. I needed to slow down and think like a cop. Teresa might know where they were. I set off for her house.

Since the day before, someone had festooned the drab duplex's front porch with colored lights. I could hear laughter inside, and music that my untutored ear identified as mariachi. I wondered if the doorbell could be heard over the party noise, but the door swung open to reveal Teresa, transformed by makeup, a sparkly top and black velour leggings, hair glistening in elaborate curls piled on top of her head. Her welcoming smile vanished when she recognized me.

"Hi, Teresa. I was looking for Frank, but he's not home. Do you know where I could find him?" The way she pulled the door partly closed behind her gave me a clue. "Is he here?"

Teresa frowned. "What you want with him? You saw him yesterday. He don't have no more to say to you."

"I just want to ask a couple of questions. I think the police might have missed something about his mother's death and—"

"Stop hassling him! He don't need more trouble!" she hissed, scanning the road behind me. I half-turned to see what she was looking for.

"You think the gangs are still after him?" I gasped.

"Gangs? You don't know nothing! You think *gangs* killed his mom?" she sneered, this suddenly adult woman schooling me, a veteran detective. She was right: I knew nothing about Frank's life, his fears and struggles. Like most cops, I relied on assumptions about Latinos, the homeless, addicts—assumption being a polite word for profiling. Latino meant gang, either gang member or gang victim. And I'd ignored the harm my presence in his neighborhood might cause. If Marta had been killed for calling out a drug dealer, her son might also be a target.

I nodded, absorbing Teresa's anger. "Look, can you give him this?" I pulled the envelopes containing the gift cards from my pocket. "For Christmas. I bought a gift card for Gloria too. I haven't any idea what she'd like. Perhaps you could help her spend it?"

Teresa shuffled the envelopes, looking at the name on each. She seemed to soften. "Yeah, okay. Thanks."

"Would you ask Frank to call me? I've written my phone number on the back of the envelope. No pressure. I just want to help." A reluctant nod. I headed back to my car, turning on the sidewalk to see Teresa silhouetted in the rainbow-lit doorway. "*Feliz Navidad!*" I called. She smiled, probably at my atrocious accent, then repeated the greeting back to me and disappeared inside.

On the way home, I was tempted to stop at the supermarket for a bottle of wine—it was Christmas Eve, after all. I'd already engaged the turn signal when I spotted a black-and-white in the parking lot. What if the cops recognized me? I bet I was already the object of gossip, if not ridicule, at the department. I didn't want to add to the rumor mill. I could have shopped for booze elsewhere, but as I drove on, I thought about the other ten OD files waiting at home, each one representing a life—someone's son or daughter, mother or brother. If my deeper investigation of just two files—Victoria's and Marta's—had uncovered inadequacies in the police investigation, shouldn't I stay sober to continue my research?

After I pulled into my designated space, I sat in the dim quiet of the parking garage under my building, listening to the tick of the cooling engine. I'd been spinning like an angry top, using cynicism as a shield as I careened against obstacles. My obsession with Victoria—yes, I could see now that perhaps it was an obsession—had knocked me sideways. Self-medicating with alcohol hadn't helped. It had taken a total flame-out—my enforced medical leave—to force me to reassess. I had a purpose. For the first time in a while, I could lift my eyes to the horizon, daring to imagine a future with me in it. Perhaps back with the department, perhaps not. But productive, working cases, seeking the truth, seeking justice. I wasn't out of the woods yet; my hold on this new perspective was tenuous. The way my anger flared at minor setbacks, and my need to schedule every hour with activity demonstrated that. Could I ever peel back the layers of hurt and find inner peace? My feisty abrasive persona, developed over a lifetime, gave a snort of derision at such a New Age thought. I'd be lighting scented candles and practicing mindfulness next.

The car had cooled to silence. I climbed out and took the elevator up to my apartment.

****

I put Marta Gutierrez's file aside for now. Until Frank called me there was little more I could do. Next in the file pile was Justine Norman, the nurse from Denver, visiting family in Coalport. She had been found dead at the hotel where Marta worked on November 1st, eighteen days after Victoria's death. The file had similar cursory investigation notes to Marta's: a statement from the hotel maid who found the body, electronic keycard record showing no other entry to her room after she checked in and went upstairs, and confirmation of identity by a sister who lived in town. The sister's statement included the fact that Justine had an early flight back to Denver the next day, explaining why she chose to spend her last night at the hotel rather than with relatives. I saw no evidence of an inquiry into where she'd obtained the drugs that killed her.

The autopsy summary was more useful. Besides the fentanyl, there were traces of another opiate—oxycontin—in her system, as well as needle marks between her toes. A search of her effects had turned up a small vial with traces of oxy inside. The container was labeled with the name of the Denver hospital where Justine had worked. I knew medical professionals had a high rate of drug addiction, and I bet Myers, the detective on the case, knew that too. He wouldn't have spent much time looking for foul play. Another addict miscalculated the dose and paid the price. He would have sent a copy of the file to Denver P.D. for follow-up, and then closed the case.

But why fentanyl? Had Justine run out of her drug of choice, and gone looking for a local source? Her sister might have more information. I made a note of the sister's name and address, and cursed Christmas again. I'd have to wait until the holiday was over to go interview her. I had days to while away with housework and laundry until I could follow the lead. At least I had my statue for company.

Chapter 23

John was glad of the thirty-minute drive to his home out in the county: time to think about his meeting with Christine and the conversation with Edgar Luchinski. Christine had liked the statue, and he gave himself a pat on the back for selecting the right gift. Her initial coldness had receded somewhat. He hoped she would change her mind about Christmas dinner with Ed and Perry. It would do her good to get out of the apartment. He didn't like to think of her alone, brooding about her enforced leave of absence. She hadn't reacted to the news that Luchinski now agreed there was something off about Victoria Hartman's death—that the overdose might not be suicide. Perhaps that meant she had finally gotten over her obsession. He was less confident that she had forgiven him for sharing his concerns about her mental health with Kleinberg. He wasn't convinced his conversation with the captain had caused her suspension from duty—Christine and Kleinberg were on a collision course anyway—but it had felt good to apologize.

More worrying was the idea that he might have missed something in the autopsy of Victoria's body. He'd boasted to Christine he'd done hundreds of autopsies in the past, but that had been in a hospital setting training medical students, not as part of a criminal inquiry. The cause of death in those cases was usually evident. As a medical examiner, more was asked of him—he needed to go deeper than the obvious. The boy this morning, for example—should he have gone to the boy's home to examine the body *in situ* to more accurately determine time and place of death, rather than rely on the distraught mother's statement that her son had been fine when he'd gone up to his room at nine the previous evening? But the police had already authorized the removal of the boy's body to the morgue before he was involved.

The light was fading when John reached his house. After turning on a few lights, he poured himself a scotch, fired up his laptop and accessed the M.E. office site. The report on fentanyl deaths he'd given to Captain Kleinberg needed updating with the autopsy data about the boy. When he had completed the task, John leaned back, sipping his drink and considering the spreadsheet on the screen. Following the drug task force protocols, the data included all fentanyl overdose deaths in the county in the last six months, the name, gender and age of the deceased, and the date, time and place the corpse had been found. There were now thirteen names on the list. After twenty minutes of keyboard activity, John created another spreadsheet: *all* drug overdose deaths in the county in the last six months. Twenty names, including the thirteen from the first spreadsheet, now appeared. Victoria Hartman was one of the additional seven.

Playing with the data—sorting and ranking to try and find connections or clusters around the time or place of death, or the gender or age of the deceased—turned up nothing. The deaths seemed randomly scattered on all parameters, except for the fact of a drug overdose uniting them. He would have to go back and review each detailed autopsy report with a fresh eye. That might take days. Well, he was off duty until the twenty-ninth. He'd start with Victoria Hartman.

Victoria Hartman was different from most of the others. She had not injected street drugs, but had instead ingested prescription medications. The body had been clean, well-nourished. He usually relied on the statements of police at the scene when interpreting his autopsy findings. If the responding officers or assigned detective reported the deceased was a known addict, or had prior drug convictions, John didn't go out of his way to look for other possible causes of death. If the body evidenced contusions, or foreign DNA was found, he tended to put it down to the drug user's lifestyle, not to possible foul play. In Victoria's case, his assumptions were based not on police reports but on information from Dr. Luchinski about Victoria's underlying disease. He had been familiar with Luchinski's reputation and read papers he had authored on hematology. When Luchinski had suggested suicide, John had deferred to the other doctor's expertise and familiarity with his patient. When, that morning, the doctor expressed doubts about the cause of death, John was ready to defer to him again. Of course, Christine had voiced the same suspicions months earlier, but she'd been so wrapped up in her fascination with the dead doppelgänger that he'd discounted the theory that Victoria had been murdered. Maybe he should talk to her about the November trip to Philadelphia and find out what she'd discovered there, but first he'd revisit the autopsy report in light of Luchinski's call.

The report noted slight *ante mortem* bruising on the upper right arm in two places about eight centimeters apart, each bruise was less than two centimeters across. He had remarked that PNH—paroxysmal nocturnal hemoglobinuria—might make the patient susceptible to bruising. Victoria suffered from PNH, therefore John had concluded his analysis without inquiring further into how the oedema occurred or estimating the length of time between occurrence and death. He examined the color photographs included with the report—hard to tell if the marks were more red than blue. His best guess now was that the bruising occurred anywhere between eighteen and two hours before death. It struck him that eight centimeters is the average grip between thumb and fingers: someone may have grasped Victoria's upper arm to hold or drag her, but there was nothing to show a causal connection with her death.

He turned to the section on DNA analysis. A base sample of Victoria's DNA was extracted from the inside of her mouth for matching purposes. Following protocols, swabs were then taken from under the fingernails. The samples showed no foreign DNA. John stared at the results for several minutes, trying to identify what nagged at him. Then he saw it: not only was there no foreign DNA under the fingernails, there was nothing at all. Unless Victoria had been wearing latex gloves, or scoured her hands with a powerful cleansing agent afterwards, some traces of the drugs she had ingested to kill herself would have remained on her hands, as well as other detritus of everyday living: dust, fibers, skin particles. Another scenario began to suggest itself. Perhaps Victoria had been overcome by someone who had forced her to swallow the drugs, then her attacker erased any signs of struggle by cleaning her hands and under her fingernails. Perhaps there had been two assailants, she had been threatened with a gun, or a fast-acting drug like Rohypnol or GHB had been used to control her.

John shook his head to dislodge these farfetched ideas. Wasn't it still more likely that Victoria had committed suicide in a temporary fit of depression? Perhaps she'd found out the son she was searching for was dead, or she had found him and he had rejected her approaches? Yet the fact remained he had not pursued other possibilities, no matter how unlikely. He had not followed up on the bruising or the unnatural cleanliness of the hands.

With an uneasy feeling, John began going through the autopsies performed on the other overdose cases. By 2 a.m. on the morning of Christmas Day, he had filled several pages of a notebook with questions he had failed to ask at the time of the autopsy. The concern Luchinski had aroused about Victoria's death had deepened into a pervasive self-doubt.

Chapter 24

I woke the next morning with a sour feeling of dread. I was staring at my face in the bathroom mirror before I identified its origin: Christmas Day. I'd probably spent Christmas Day alone as often as I had with family or friends, yet this year was different. The aloneness possessed a quality of rejection and failure, as if I was the only person excluded from the festivities. I tried to shake it off and recapture the feeling of purpose I'd experienced the day before, but it was no good. Christmas Day stretched out like a desert in front of me, without the possibility of any advance in my investigation. Although it was not yet nine, I felt the urgent need for a drink. A run might purge the urge.

I ran-walked-ran for an hour, until my body dripped with sweat and my lungs were bursting. When I returned to the apartment, I decided to give myself a spa day to pass the time. I filled the bathtub, searching in vain at the back of the vanity for any perfumed bath oil I might have purchased or purloined in a forgotten life. I had to settle for baking soda, which the legend on the box assured me would soothe and soften the skin. Perhaps it had been in the fridge too long, because there was no noticeable effect. I shaved my legs, cut my toenails, trimmed my bangs, and tweezed my eyebrows, stopping just short of a Thirties Hollywood star's look of permanent surprise. I dressed in black, which suited my mood. And it was still only eleven-thirty.

The convenience store a block over was owned and operated by East Indians; they would stay open on the holiday. The wine selection there was probably not extensive, but at this point I thought anything alcoholic would do. The voices of my better angels argued the craving was a test of my willpower, and I shouldn't give up the progress I'd made over the last days. I was hunting for my wallet, the fading voices of the angel choir overcome by my impeccable reasoning that I deserved a drink after all I'd been through, when my phone rang.

John. Should I answer? I was still mad at him for interfering in my life, but he *had* given me the mysteriously powerful statue that now stood in my living room. Would *she* want me to answer? Would Victoria? I thought of those bracelets evangelical Christians wear: WWJD—what would Jesus do? Shit, I *was* going crazy! Answer the damn phone!

"Hi, Christine, Merry Christmas!" John sounded upbeat.

I bristled. "Yeah, same to you," I replied, keeping my voice flat.

John didn't seem to notice. "I wondered whether I could change your mind about going to Ed and Perry's party. They'd love to see you, and there's no need to bring anything—they adore entertaining, and they've been preparing for weeks. It's just a few neighbors and a friend visiting from California."

There'd be alcohol there. The thought flashed through my mind, followed by another: I hate parties. But perhaps today a party was what I needed to dispel my depression.

"What time?" I asked, not committing myself.

"Three-ish. Time to mingle before they serve dinner about five. I can come and pick you up—"

"No! I'll drive myself." If I was going, I wanted to be in control of my own transportation. Then I could escape if I needed to.

"Okay, let me give you the address, and I'll meet you there. Do you have a pen?"

I wrote down the address and John's directions for finding the house. After all, it wouldn't hurt to have an option if my own company became too appalling.

****

From the outside, Ed and Perry's house looked like a typical ranch-style home, but when I nudged open the front door which had been left hospitably ajar, I saw that interior renovation had created an expansive entertaining space. The foyer opened onto a large room with a wall of windows facing east. About a dozen guests, glasses in hand, were standing in chattering groups, laughter rising above the background conversation. I thought about creeping out again. I'd changed my mind a dozen times about coming.

Ed and Perry seemed a unit—EdandPerry—but they were physical opposites, Ed being tall and slim with movie-star good looks—a kind of aging Cary Grant, he even had a faux British accent. Perry was short, plump, and Jewish. It was Perry who noticed me first and hurried forward to greet me, a champagne flute in each hand. John must have been keeping an eye out because he was close behind.

"Welcome!" Perry proffered one of the glasses to me.

"Ah…I'm not drinking for now," I said, blushing scarlet to the roots of my hair. Why was I so embarrassed about it? It wasn't as if I had declared myself a hopeless alcoholic. I sensed John's head swiveling to look at me, but Perry didn't think it was a big deal. He thrust the flute at John and seized my arm with his free hand.

"Come and meet our dear friend Gabby, bartender to the stars. She makes the most divine mocktails."

I was swept off to the makeshift bar at one end of the room. John, a glass in each hand, stared after me.

"Gabrielle, meet Christine. Give her one of those concoctions you served us last night." With a grin, he left to circulate amongst the other guests.

"Do you like cranberries?" Gabby was tall and slim, with a California tan and blonde hair. I should hate her, but she seemed friendly.

"I haven't thought about it," I replied. "Are you really the bartender to the stars?"

She laughed. "No, I just tend bar two or three nights a week in L.A. to pay the rent. I'm a screenwriter—or at least I want to be." She was pouring from various bottles into a cocktail shaker. "What do you do?"

"I'm a…detective." My reply was hesitant but she didn't pick up on it. "Are you sure that's non-alcoholic?" I gestured towards the wine-dark, frothy confection she was pouring into a coupe. She floated a mint leaf on the top.

"Better be," she said. "I've been sober for five years, and I just drank one."

"Oh. Isn't it difficult, working in a bar and not drinking?" This was direct even for me, but I was curious.

"I like to think watching all the drunks make fools of themselves reinforces my sobriety, but honestly, staying sober's difficult wherever you are."

That made sense. I liked this woman.

John appeared at my side. He had managed to down the champagne and get rid of the glass. "Gin and tonic, please," he said addressing Gabrielle. I smirked; he had taken her for the hired help—how embarrassing. I wasn't going to help him.

"Yes, sir. Do you have a preference of gin?" Gabby played her part demurely.

John caught sight of my face and realized his mistake. "Oh, I'm so sorry—I didn't—I mean I thought you…"

Gabby and I cracked up. John flushed, then joined half-heartedly in the laughter.

"Gabby's a screenwriter in Hollywood," I told him, promoting my new friend's status from wannabe to potential Oscar winner. "And John cuts up dead bodies—he's the Medical Examiner," I added for Gabrielle's benefit.

I'd have liked to chat with Gabby a while longer, but when other people came to refill their glasses, John took me aside.

"I wanted to talk to you about some old cases—drug overdose deaths."

"Oh?" I was wary. Had he found out about the files I'd taken from the police department? How?

"Yes. I keep the drug task force updated on autopsies where the cause of death is fentanyl overdose. The numbers are mounting—it's disturbing. Yesterday, I did an autopsy on a sixteen-year-old boy."

I nodded, unsure where this was headed. In the past, he'd seemed detached about the bodies he examined, regardless of their age or situation. I found it hard to believe his compassion had been awakened by one teenager. And why was he speaking to me about it? Yes, he knew I'd been seconded to the task force, but he also knew I was now on indefinite leave.

"So I pulled up the autopsy reports on ODs going back before the Coalport P.D. joined the task force—deaths in the last six months," John continued. "Including Victoria Hartman's."

He stopped talking, wanting my reaction. I needed to tread carefully. "Did you reach any conclusions?"

"Yes. I've been doing a shitty job."

I gasped. This was the last thing I expected him to say.

"In my defense, I was new in the job, there was a backlog, the detectives seemed content with my reports—I know, I know, poor excuses." He threw back the rest of his drink, looking around the room to avoid my astonished gaze.

"So…what are you going to do?" I asked. "Those cases are closed. Good luck getting Kleinberg to reopen them without new evidence." Or even with new evidence, I thought. He'd dismissed the facts I'd turned up about Victoria as a fantasy.

"I wondered, now you have some time on your hands, whether you might help me look into these cases, you know, like you did with Victoria's. Maybe between us we can do a more thorough investigation."

I felt an urge to laugh—not at John: I felt sorry for him. It must have cost him dearly to admit professional fault. My amusement—almost hysteria—was at the situation. At that moment, most of the files he was referring to were spread across my dining table. I had already made a good start at digging out the truth behind Marta Gutierrez's death, and forged some connection—

the airport hotels—with two other cases. However, I was a disgraced cop on leave because of my mental instability. Even if I could solve these crimes, who was going to listen to me? But John's credibility was impeccable. He had the respect of the police department. He also had access to databases and insider information off-limits to me. The practical advantages of assisting John to make amends for prior oversights was attractive.

"What do you think?" John's face was abject, his voice plaintive.

I hesitated. John was all humility now, but his need to be in control was innate. How long before his aura of superiority would drive me over the edge? Plus, he was a rules follower: what would he think about me stealing files and taking them home with me?

"I don't mind taking a look—kicking around some ideas with you. As you say, I don't have anything else to do at the moment."

Chapter 25

I agreed to meet John for lunch the next day to discuss Victoria's case. He was pretty wasted by the end of the party, and I wondered if he'd be so eager to rehash the shortcomings of his autopsy report when he sobered up. Sharing my discovery about her stay at the hotel at the airport might persuade him to pressure Kleinberg to look at the case again. But even if John were to use his access and credibility on Victoria's behalf, I doubted the captain would budge. The whole department was focused on nailing the big players in the fentanyl smuggling and distribution racket, with no time or manpower to devote to the unrelated death of a woman who had no friends or relatives hassling them for answers.

However, before my lunchtime rendezvous, I had other matters to deal with. Denver was an hour ahead of the West Coast, so I started working the phones at eight a.m. After several false starts, I reached a person of sufficient authority in the Human Resources department of the hospital where Justine Norman worked.

Introducing myself as a recruiter for the fictional Northwest Mercy Clinic, I asked about a reference for their employee, Justine Norman, R.N.

"We don't give job references over the phone."

I had anticipated this. Of course, if I'd been calling in a law enforcement role, the pleasant-voiced HR director would have been only too happy to help with my investigation, but that approach was off-limits. "I understand. Perhaps you could just confirm the fact of Justine Norman's employment as an R.N. in your hospital?"

A pause while the woman considered my more reasonable request. I heard the clack of computer keys.

"We have no one of that name currently employed here."

The slight emphasis on "currently" gave me the opening I needed. "Ah, I see. Can you tell me whether Ms. Norman is eligible for rehire?" I thought about adding, *as one HR professional to another*, but that wasn't necessary.

"No, she is not."

"Thank you so much. You have a nice day now!" I grinned as I disconnected. I knew enough HR-speak to interpret the information: Justine had been fired, and given the nursing shortage, probably for something pretty serious—like stealing hospital supplies of oxycontin to feed her habit.

I checked the address Justine's sister had given when identifying the body: a new suburb of middle-class family homes on the edge of Coalport. Sipping a second cup of coffee, I planned my strategy. The neighborhood called for conservative clothes: a blazer and tailored pants. I was pleased I now needed only the minimum of concealer on my bruised eye—clean living helps you heal faster. I wished my beat-up compact sedan wasn't quite so streaked with mud and rain, but there was no time for a carwash.

The front yard at the home of Jessica Devry *née* Norman was neatly kept although winter-bare, and the house windows shone. I applied myself to the bellpush and heard a muted *bing-bong*. Footsteps. A woman my age, dressed in pink designer sweats, opened the door.

"Good morning. Jessica Devry?" She nodded, her expression friendly. "I'm so sorry to disturb you during the holidays, but we're investigating the epidemic of recent fentanyl overdoses in this region. You may have heard of the Inter-Agency Drug Task Force?" A frown replaced the pleasant regard, but I plowed on. "I have some questions about your sister's tragic death. I wonder if I could have a few minutes of your time?"

"I already gave a statement. I don't know where she got the drugs."

I sensed she was considering closing the door, but politeness held her back. I had to take advantage of the hesitation. "I'm so sorry for your loss. This epidemic is heartbreaking. Just before Christmas, a local boy—high school basketball star—died from a fentanyl overdose. So many lives needlessly lost. We're trying to find some connection between the victims that might lead us to the criminals responsible. There may be details you can provide that can help us. It'll only take a few minutes."

Jessica indicated I should follow her inside. Victory! We entered an open-plan living area as tidy as the front yard. I walked over to some framed photographs on a shelf. Most featured a boy at various ages up to early teens. "Your son?"

"Yes. It's his dad's turn for Christmas. He'll be home tomorrow." That explained the lack of mess. "Would you like a coffee, water, anything?"

"Oh, no, thanks, I'm fine. May I sit?"

"Of course. What did you want to ask?"

Ice broken, Jessica appeared eager to tell me about

her younger sister. How she had shown such promise, how proud the family was of her choice of career. Her parents still lived in Denver where the girls grew up. "Then gradually, Justine seemed to pull away. Mom and Dad didn't see her for months at a time. She never answered my calls and texts. When she asked to come and stay here, I knew something bad had happened."

"She'd been fired," I supplied in a soft voice.

"Yes! I didn't know why at first. She applied for nursing jobs here but kept getting rejected. She was so nervous all the time, on edge. When I found out she was on drugs—*that* was why she'd been fired—I tried to get her into a program. She refused. I couldn't have her staying here with Colin—I could lose custody! We had a big fight. She was going to go back to Denver…"

"Other than you and Colin, who did she spend time with while she was here?"

Jessica shrugged. "I don't know. I'm at work during the day, and Colin's at school. She went out for walks, she said. Sometimes she'd grocery shop for me or pick up Colin from school if he had practice."

"What school does he go to?"

"Parkview High. He's a freshman."

I made a few notes. "Any idea where she obtained the drugs? Did she bring a supply with her from Denver, or did she get them locally?"

"Well, I'm pretty sure she ran out of whatever she brought with her, because she pestered me to get her an appointment with my doctor—said she had a back injury. She saw him a week before she died, but I don't think he prescribed what she wanted, because that's when we had the argument and she booked a flight back to Denver."

"Do you know why she chose to stay at that

particular hotel?"

She shook her head. "I said I didn't mind getting up early and driving her to the airport. To be honest, I wanted to make sure she left. She said no, she'd found some deal."

I raised my eyebrows at that.

"Oh, I assumed she meant a deal on the room. You think she met a drug dealer at the hotel?"

My turn to shrug. "It's a possibility. Is there anything else she said or did that might be significant? Anything at all?"

Jessica pondered. "Nothing *she* said, but I was thinking about that boy you said ODed on fentanyl. What high school did he go to?"

I didn't know; John had just mentioned the boy's death in passing.

Jessica continued, "Something Colin mentioned—a couple of times, when Justine picked him up from school, she was talking to some guys. Colin noticed because they had a really cool car—he was impressed. He's crazy about cars, can't wait to get his permit."

I thought of Frank Gutierrez's comment about the "white guys, nice cars" hanging around after practice. Frank didn't go to Parkview, but the technique of recruiting customers for drugs outside schools wouldn't be restricted to one high school. Perhaps they'd identified Justine as a potential distributor, someone to extend the network to Denver. I shouldn't get ahead of myself. "Maybe other parents picking up their kids?" I suggested.

"I didn't get that impression."

I probed, hoping to get more details, but I could see Jessica was disappearing down a mental rabbit hole, imagining her son being enticed into a cool car by drug dealers. I attempted to reassure her, explaining the task force was making great progress in tracing the fentanyl supply, but the worried look in her eyes told me Colin would not be leaving the house unaccompanied for a while.

Chapter 26

John felt weirdly nervous as he waited for Christine at the diner. When he thought back over the ups and downs of their relationship, he had to question why he'd want to get involved with her again. Back in October— had it really only been two months?—he'd found her independent spirit attractive. Then independence began to look like stubbornness, even willfulness. Watching her mess up had been hard, but he'd kept his distance. He'd promised himself when he moved here that he'd keep life simple, no entanglements. Ironic that now she seemed to be pulling herself together, *he* was mired in self-doubt.

When Nancy left him back in Tucson, he'd felt hurt. He hadn't seen her defection coming and it had been a shock. But he never blamed himself. Nancy changed; she started to want different things than he did, but that wasn't *his* fault. Their parting had been civilized; no recriminations on either part. Christine, in contrast, had the knack of making him feel guilty, as if he was responsible for her screw-ups. Perhaps it was the difference in their ages, or the fact she had no family or friend network to support her. She would hate to see herself as vulnerable, but in truth she was. On reflection, his current discomfort might be explained by the unaccustomed urge to protect Christine. He'd never felt protective toward anyone in the past, and knew the last thing she wanted was his protection. What to do? Stay close to Christine, trying to hide the ache he felt every time he saw her? Or walk away now, and preserve his autonomy?

Too late: he was on the point of leaving when Christine entered the restaurant. The low winter sun gave a golden glow to her face. On cue the ache returned.

She was neatly dressed in a blazer and pants rather than her usual jeans and leather jacket.

"You look nice. Interview with your bank manager?"

Christine laughed but didn't answer. They ordered, and while waiting for their food, discussed the party the previous evening.

"I'm afraid I made an ass of myself," John admitted. "Too much alcohol on an empty stomach, and I hadn't slept much the night before."

"Hmm, so those apologies for ignoring my suspicions about Victoria's death were just the booze talking?"

"Definitely not. I want to re-examine the case, and I think there may be others I need to look at again. I need your help because I'm still unfamiliar with police procedures—what I should rely on from the police file, and what I need to question."

Christine looked at him askance. "You think I can be objective?"

"Look, I know you've been critical of your colleagues. Perhaps that's what's needed: an unsympathetic eye. Let's start with Victoria Hartman and see where we go. Tell me again what you found out in Philadelphia."

Christine sighed. After taking a moment to organize

her thoughts, she laid out what Frances Bell had said about Victoria making a fresh start, her suspicions regarding the Ditton Foundation, and what she had learned subsequently from James Anderson about Victoria's parentage and her teen pregnancy. "I'm convinced that Victoria located Gaston and came here to meet her son. He's a few months shy of his eighteenth birthday. With her inheritance, she could make a new life with him. All the secrecy suggests she knew someone didn't want that to happen."

John nodded, absorbing the information. "That's persuasive but all circumstantial. In my view, the most convincing evidence of foul play is the way her hands and fingernails were cleaned." He had missed that in his autopsy report, and the realization hurt.

"Yes, but there's more." Christine described the hotel desk clerk's identification of Victoria as a guest who had reserved two rooms for three nights but checked out early. "If we could review the lobby security camera videos, we'd know who she was with when she checked out. Maybe she didn't leave the hotel voluntarily."

"How can we get hold of those videos?" John asked. The idea of becoming involved in detection outside the clinical laboratory setting was starting to entice him.

"The drug task force already has them. A Canadian drug kingpin called Larry Cremond was staying at the same hotel as Victoria." Christine was watching him with an intensity he couldn't read.

"Perhaps I could get Captain Kleinberg to let me have a look?" The request would be way outside his remit, but his relationship with the captain was good. John could explain he was professionally interested in getting a broader understanding of criminal detective work.

"That's a great idea, John." Christine smiled. For a second he considered whether she was manipulating him, then dismissed it.

Chapter 27

The moment I left John in the restaurant I had second thoughts about encouraging him to view the hotel security videos. What if Kleinberg guessed that I had suggested the idea? That might convert my indefinite leave to permanent. What if John couldn't spot Victoria Hartman or Gaston on the videos? He wasn't used to sitting in front of a screen for hours, eyes focused, mind cleared of all distractions, so that when that one anomaly—something just a bit off—came up, you recognized it at once. If only I could be there! But then I checked myself: I couldn't afford to disappear down that rabbit hole again, chasing Victoria through conspiracy plots fueled by alcohol and bad dreams. I was making good progress on the other files, being a good cop, following leads that should have been explored in the initial investigations. I should keep my head down and stick to the routine I'd established.

But what had I accomplished really? When I thought about it, I'd gathered no compelling evidence on either Marta Gutierrez or Justine Norman that would reverse the finding of accidental overdose. Even if I had, they were still dead, their families still grieving. All I had done was keep myself busy—distracted from my failures and self-destructive impulses.

I'd been walking aimlessly, caught up in the hamster wheel of my own miserable thoughts. When at last I looked around me, I was disoriented. I must have walked right past my parked car. I didn't recognize the deserted, rundown street. I was lost. The sun had disappeared behind heavy clouds, and my smart tailored jacket offered no warmth. Shivering, I tried to think how long it had been since leaving the restaurant, how far I might have come, and whether I'd made any turns. Think, girl, think! But I was stuck in a spiral of negativity: I was a mess, a loser, a screw-up. My head was full of Kleinberg barking at me, John scolding me, Myers taunting me. Somewhere in the mix, my parents' disgust.

I couldn't stay here, but I couldn't think what direction to go. A sign across the street: flickering blue neon, the only movement and color in the drab neighborhood. The sputtering letters dragged me forward like a lighthouse in a storm. A bitter laugh escaped me. Somehow I'd found my way back to the scene of my greatest humiliation: the bar where I had gotten drunk, been slugged unconscious, and picked up by the cops. Perfect! The circle was complete. I might have fooled myself for a while that I was walking a straight line, but I was doomed to repeat the cycle of my past defeats.

I pushed open the heavy door, feeling drained. Taking a seat at the bar, I saw the same unfriendly bartender mopping the same far section of the counter.

"Vodka, please. Straight up."

****

An hour later, I left the bar. The alcohol had done the job demanded of it: drowning panic and replacing it with reckless self-confidence. I half-expected to find the bearded thug and his skinny girlfriend still arguing in the alley. This time, I'd deflect his right hook and floor the guy. But the streets were empty, winter dusk already turning into night. I could see my breath when I exhaled, while the alcohol in my system kept me from feeling cold. I pointed myself in the direction from which I thought I'd come and started the unsteady trek back to my car.

A block later I heard a buzz. My brain took a moment to identify the sound of the phone in my pocket. I extracted it but couldn't make out the caller's identity: the screen was hazy.

" 'Lo?"

"Hi, McQuarry. It's Myers."

I said nothing. Silenced by surprise, but also suspecting I wouldn't be able to control the slurring of my words.

"Look, I know you're mad at Kleinberg, and me too probably, but I wanted to talk to you about something. Can you meet me? My shift ends at seven."

I ran my tongue around my mouth and concentrated on speaking clearly. "What about?"

"It's about that tip you gave us—Larry Cremond staying at that airport hotel. I'll explain when I see you. Can you make it to the coffee shop on Tenth Street at, say, seven-thirty?"

I thought about it. Myers wasn't a friend. He wasn't calling to thank me for the tip, or to console me for being kicked out of the department. He needed something from me. Did I want to help him? No, but I was intrigued. "I'm on medical leave. Hadn't you heard?"

"Yeah, this is unofficial. Kleinberg doesn't need to know."

"Huh. Okay, I'll listen, but don't count on me to do your job for you. I'm on leave, remember?"

I had less than three hours to sober up. After twenty frustrating minutes searching along streets lined with parked cars, I found my car and drove slowly, carefully, home. I drank a pint glass of cold water, put a pot of coffee on to brew, and took a long shower. By the time I dried off and downed some caffeine, my head was clearer—throbbing, but clearer. Did I have time for a nap? I couldn't risk falling asleep and not waking up until the early hours, so I drank more coffee, ate a sandwich, and thumbed through the files again until it was time to leave.

Myers was sitting at the rear of the coffee shop with his back against the wall: typical cop defensive position. The only other customer was leaving as I entered. I walked straight past the barista—I was sufficiently caffeinated, thank you—and took a seat beside him, requiring him to twist sideways to talk to me.

"Hi, McQuarry. How's it going?"

Not inclined to waste time on pleasantries, I asked, "So what's this about?"

"You remember you told Kleinberg the desk clerk at the hotel identified Larry Cremond from a photo array you showed her?"

I nodded.

"Well, we got the registration records—everyone who stayed there from September until Thanksgiving. Guess what? No Larry Cremond." I showered and changed for this?

"Probably used a false name," I said in the acid-sweet tones of a first-grade teacher.

"Yeah, that's what we thought," Myers replied. "We had the security video too, just from the beginning of October; they delete the data after a couple of months.

We shared it with the Mounties. Cremond's their suspect, and they'd be better at picking him out. Plus it's a shitload of work—they're still going through it all."

I tapped my fingers on the table, substituting pissed-off principal for first-grade teacher. "Myers, get to the point."

The barista called over, "We close in twenty minutes."

Myers waved an acknowledgment, then turned back to me. "Anyway, I had some time on my hands so I decided to have a look." He stared at me, jaw clenched, eyebrows lowered, waiting for me to say something. What? I gazed back blankly. "The security camera's behind the reception desk. It captures everyone who checks in." He paused again. "October eleven, four p.m. *You* checked in." He leaned back with a smirk of satisfaction.

"It wasn't me."

Myers ignored me. "What's your game, McQuarry? Want all the glory for yourself? Think you can crack the case without the team?"

"It wasn't me." I kept my voice level, but I was beginning to simmer.

He talked over my voice. "Or are you part of it? In on the drug smuggling? Larry Cremond's cover?"

"Listen to me, you pea-brained schmuck!" I'd reached boiling point. "It wasn't me, it was Victoria Hartman, the overdose victim we had a hard time identifying. She was my doppelgänger. If you don't believe me, ask the M.E. He's the one that spotted the likeness." I had been about to add, "Look at the photo in her file," before I remembered I'd purloined her file along with several others when I left the department.

173

I didn't think Myers was familiar with the term "doppelgänger." His jaw was working as he tried to come up with another attack. I forestalled him. "You checked the hotel register for October eleventh, right? Saw her name? Two rooms for three nights? Who was with her?"

He back-pedaled now, looking for an out. "I was looking for drug dealers, not sad little suicides. Her name as a guest didn't mean anything to me. The video—"

"—Was Victoria checking in. Who was with her?"

The barista looked worried as the volume of our argument rose. I willed her to call the police on us; that would serve Myers right. "Was there a kid, a boy about seventeen years old?"

"No! You were alone—"

"*Victoria* was alone."

"Yeah," Myers deflated like a punctured balloon.

"Maybe you'd better go back and look at the video again, because Victoria was supposed to be meeting her son, who she hadn't seen since he was a newborn. She'd searched and saved and planned for this reunion, and two days later she's dead. I think that's strange, don't you?"

He shrugged. "Maybe the son didn't show."

"Maybe *you* need to do your job." I stood and made for the door, stopping when I reached it to call back, "And let me know what you find out."

I let the door slam behind me. Besides feeling like shit—head exploding, jittery from the coffee, and nauseous from the sandwich I'd forced down—I was smiling. If I knew Myers and his competitive streak, he'd rush back to scrutinize the video again. Perhaps he'd solve the mystery of the early checkout: when and how had Victoria left the building? With luck, there'd be a clear image of Gaston coming across the lobby, proving my theory that they'd met up at the hotel. Of course, Myers would want to steal the glory of uncovering a murder that had been wrongly dismissed as a suicide. I didn't care. I should link him up with John—two male egos are better than one. Together, they'd have no difficulty persuading Kleinberg to reopen the case.

Meanwhile, I needed to climb back on the wagon, the horse, the bicycle, or whatever means of locomotion had been carrying me soberly forward. I still had leads to follow up.

Chapter 28

I slept fitfully and woke early. Having endured the worst of the hangover the evening before, my head was clear. I lay under the covers, making a mental list of things to do, including calling John to make sure he didn't blunder into Kleinberg's office, requesting to see the hotel security video—I was pretty sure Myers would follow up on that. Then I remembered with a jolt of adrenalin that James Anderson would be back at work today. Partnering with a geezer twice my age whose website featured fishing stories felt strange, but he was as determined to uncover the truth about Victoria's death as I was. Plus, he didn't let his ego get in the way.

I armed myself with coffee before I dialed Anderson's number at nine-thirty East Coast time. He answered on the first ring. After I announced myself, I plunged in. "I'm calling to see how you got on with Andrea Faber at the Ditton Foundation."

"Ah, yes. Victoria Hartman." He wasn't going to be rushed. I could hear papers shuffling as he continued, "How was your Christmas? Relaxing, I hope?"

"Yes, fine. Were you able to find out anything?"

"Not at first. Ms. Faber denied the foundation had anything to do with private adoptions. She's only been there a few years, so she wouldn't have been personally involved with Victoria's situation, but her demeanor was strange: edgy and nervous."

"I noticed the same thing. I thought perhaps she'd seen something in the files…"

"Hmm. I called Jerome Pinter. He's the attorney for the Ditton Foundation. He knew old Nathaniel Ditton, whom we now know was Victoria's real father. I thought he'd be able to apply some pressure."

I knew I had to let the old man tell the tale in his own way, but I clenched my fists in impatience. "Did Pinter get her to talk?"

"Turns out Jerome had his suspicions about Victoria's true parentage all along, although his law firm had no involvement in her placement with the Hartmans back in 1986." Anderson paused to cover the phone and greet someone who had entered his office before resuming, "Jerome spoke to Ms. Faber and discovered that Victoria's sizeable donation to the Foundation was in exchange for information. Jerome suspects some of that money might have been diverted into Ms. Faber's own account. He persuaded her that she could stay out of trouble if she made a full confession and the entire amount of the donation showed up in the next quarterly accounts. Once she had that assurance, she came clean, as I believe you detectives call it."

"And?" I was bouncing up and down in my chair at this point.

"She'd found some old correspondence that didn't make any sense to her until Victoria turned up asking about whether, in the past, the foundation had helped place babies for adoption. As I surmised, when his daughter became pregnant, Ted Hartman went to his old friend Nathaniel and asked for help. Nathaniel was a powerful man by this time, involved in lots of projects. There were rumors he had mob connections, but, you know, there are always rumors. Anyway, it seems Nathaniel turned to his charitable foundation to place Victoria's baby with a family in Montreal called Lemesur. There's a letter from a past executive director to the adoptive parents and their reply enclosing a check made out to the foundation."

"But Pinter told me he couldn't find any trace of the Lemesur family in Montreal," I interjected.

"With the information from their letter—the Montreal street address, and full names—we've been able to fill in the history. Gaston's adoptive mother, Amelie, died in 2013, and Gaston and his adoptive father Jean-Pierre moved to Vancouver, B.C. Victoria must have traced them there and made contact."

"Which is why she came here! The closest place in the U.S. to Vancouver! But why all the secrecy?"

"Ah. Victoria was a careful woman. I think she did some research into Jean-Pierre Lemesur, and turned up the same information as Jerome and I did: Jean-Pierre is part of a well-known Quebec crime family. His brother was jailed in 2012 for a range of offenses, which may be why Jean-Pierre left town: he might have thought he'd be next to be arrested and decided to go underground."

"Does he still go by Lemesur?" I'd have to get Myers to check the hotel guest register.

"I'm not sure. I've sent a letter certified mail to Gaston at the address I found for a J-P Lemesur in Vancouver, but it won't have been delivered yet. I was cautious in the wording, 'a bequest upon proof of identity.' If I don't hear back, I'll see about getting in touch with the local authorities or hiring a private investigator."

"I can go." The words were out of my mouth before

I considered the implications. I had no rights to operate in Canada, or in the U.S. if it came to that—I was on leave. In a confrontation with Jean-Pierre Lemesur, I couldn't call for back-up. If he or his son refused to speak to me, or even open their door, I had no recourse.

"Well, let's see what response I get to my letter first," Anderson said in his calm lawyer's voice. "Now, what have you found out at your end?"

I dragged my thoughts back to my meeting with Myers and filled Anderson in on the mounting evidence that Victoria had arranged to meet Gaston at the airport hotel. I explained the M.E.'s revised opinion regarding whether foul play might have been involved in her death. A sudden thought struck me. "Was the Lemesur crime family implicated in drug smuggling from Canada into the U.S.?"

"No idea. Why?"

"We're part of a task force investigating fentanyl smuggling from B.C. One of the drug cartel bosses was identified as staying at the same hotel as Victoria."

"A coincidence, surely?"

"Maybe."

We exchanged promises to keep each other updated on developments, and then I ended the call. I sat for a long time staring at my Cycladic-era girlfriend—yes, I had read the description of origin included in the box she came in. She stared back from the almond-shaped indentations that suggested her eyes, but she was no help in processing the various possibilities I was playing with.

How had the Lemesur father and son responded to Victoria's initial contact? Jean-Pierre might be related to criminals and not be one himself. His move to Vancouver might have been for a genuine fresh start after the tragic early death of his wife. I wondered if he had revealed to his son that he was adopted. If so, perhaps Jean-Pierre expected and welcomed Victoria's approach, another adult to help steer Gaston into adulthood, maybe contribute to college expenses, etc. And what about Gaston? Even if his family life was happy and secure, he would be curious to meet his birth mother. Her disappearance and presumed murder might have nothing to do with them, other than to multiply the tragedy of her loss.

On the other hand, if Jean-Pierre participated in his family's shady dealings, and his escape to B.C. was to evade the consequences, his son might be tainted with the same tendencies. Father and son might have avoided arrest but might still be knee-deep in crime. How would they react to Victoria? That might depend on how much she told them. If Victoria revealed that she was wealthy, they might try to take advantage of her. Worse: if she disclosed that she had made a will in Gaston's favor, that gave them a motive for murder. Both of them, or just Jean-Pierre? In my experience, seventeen years old was plenty old enough to fix character for good or ill. At about that age, I'd shrugged off all adult restraint and made my way across the country. And teenagers kill every day, recklessly or intentionally, in big city back streets or rural communities. But I couldn't imagine young Gaston acting alone.

I was desperate to grab my passport, jump in the car, and drive to Canada. If I could just eyeball the Lemesurs, I'd know whether they were responsible for Victoria's death. But I didn't have their address, and common sense told me Anderson was right: we should wait for a reply to his letter.

I had another resource: Myers. I waited until I was sure he'd be at work, then picked up my phone.

"Hey."

He recognized my voice and his reply was wary. "I'm busy. Can I call you back?"

"Nope. Just listen. While you're checking the guest register for Victoria Hartman, here's another name to look for: Lemesur, Jean-Pierre." I spelled it out for him.

"Why?"

"Gaston Lemesur is Victoria's son. He's the lad you're going to be looking for on the video. Jean-Pierre is his adoptive father. He has criminal connections. You'll want to run the name past our Canadian friends."

"I don't have time for this—"

Before he could hang up, I continued, "If it pans out, you get all the credit: a murder solved, and perhaps a lead on the fentanyl cartel. I'm on leave, remember?"

Silence. Satisfied that he'd follow up on the tip, I disconnected.

Chapter 29

John had two more days before he was due back in the office. He was sick of scrolling through old autopsy reports on the computer, noting possibilities he'd missed first time around. He decided to go for a walk in the woods. The chill would be invigorating, and perhaps exercise would help him throw off his negative mood. He pulled on some warm clothes, laced up his newly acquired hiking boots, and set out.

The problem, he was beginning to understand, was that he was a scientist through and through. He prided himself on his objectivity, only including in his findings the unambiguous facts he gleaned from the dead body in front of him—what he could see, weigh, measure. He read, but did not rely on, the first responders' reports, refusing to speculate or extrapolate on any observation he did not make for himself. That clinical approach might have worked in a university forensic laboratory, but more was required of him as Medical Examiner. To accurately determine the cause of death, he needed to understand the context and circumstances surrounding it. Not just the physical setting but the emotional dynamics—the why and how, rather than just the what. He needed empathy.

The realization pulled John up short. He'd been following a trail up through some second growth forest, the bare branches of deciduous trees outlined against a whitish sky and the groves of evergreens creating contrasting dark tunnels. He emerged at an overlook, a rocky clearing at the top of the crest. In one direction, the snow-covered peaks of the Cascades; in the other, winter-brown fields crisscrossed by roads and dotted with houses. The distant bay was masked by mist.

He stared unseeing at the view. Empathy was not his strong suit; he wondered if he was even capable of it. Had that been the root of the difficulties with Nancy? And the cause of his bungling with Christine? Could he learn empathy, like he'd studied chemistry in college? Maybe it was too late; he was too old. If so, the implications went beyond his career: he might be destined to live out his life alone, unable to sustain a relationship. He shrugged off the thought as melodramatic.

John turned to retrace his route home, meeting no one on the trail. When he had peeled off his outer clothing, he picked up the phone he'd left behind and saw a text from Christine and a voicemail from an unknown number. Christine's text was terse: "Don't worry about video. Got it covered." His jaw clenched with irritation. Typical Christine: she had to control everything herself, couldn't bear to work with anyone else. But quickly a feeling of relief superseded his exasperation. He didn't want another encounter with Kleinberg after the captain had seized on his comments to engineer Christine's removal from the department. Better to keep clear of the man for now.

The voicemail was from Detective Myers. John couldn't remember speaking with the man before, although he thought Christine had mentioned him in one of her rants about her colleagues. She'd described him as "ambitious but inept."

"Hoping you can help clear up something in connection with the Joint Drug Task Force inquiry. Back in October, a case was ruled accidental overdose, possibly suicide, but some new information's come to light. Can you give me a call?"

John jotted down Myers' number. This had to be about Victoria Hartman. The number of people who now doubted his findings in that case was growing: Christine, of course, and Dr. Luchinski; and the lawyer who'd contacted Luchinski, whose name he'd forgotten. And himself. Second-guessing himself was one thing; a careful scientist should keep an open mind. However, facing an array of sceptics was disturbing. To protect his professional reputation, he needed to get ahead of the situation. John, rather than some whistleblower, had to be the one calling for reopening the case.

He tapped Myers' number into his phone.

Chapter 30

For the next three days I waited. I waited for Myers to report on his review of the hotel lobby video, for James Anderson to call about a response to his letter to Gaston Lemesur in Vancouver, for Frank to trust me enough to talk about his mother, and for school to start again so I could scout out those "white men in fancy cars."

I hate waiting. Hanging around depending on others for action drives me crazy. I took out my frustration on the apartment: organizing closets and scrubbing those places in the bathroom and kitchen that had never seen disinfectant and sponge before. I punished my body, too, going for runs in the rain until my legs shook and my lungs were about to explode.

Catching up on what was happening in the wider world did nothing for my disposition. Usually, the period between Christmas and the New Year is a news desert, unless there's a blizzard to liven things up at the airports. This year, two mass shootings and the release of a CDC study on drug deaths filled every channel and screen. Perhaps the government hoped the study would sink without trace in the post-Christmas somnolence, but the numbers were so shocking, the report went viral in record time. Fentanyl deaths had increased by almost one thousand per cent. Pundits explained that a tiny amount of fentanyl was far more powerful than heroin, and the drug was relatively cheap and easy to manufacture. The limited availability of naloxone hydrochloride—Narcan—to reverse overdoses meant it had little effect on the numbers. I thought about the plodding efforts of our joint drug task force. Despite the dedication of resources and staff, local deaths reflected the national trend. Add hopelessness to frustration, and it was enough to drive you to drink.

At about six p.m. on New Year's Eve, a phone call from John interrupted my bleak musings.

"Christine, I need your help."

"Oh?" If he thought I would rush to volunteer my aid, he was mistaken. I would wait to see which man was calling: the vulnerable, self-flagellating John, or the egotistical, self-righteous medical examiner and general know-it-all.

"You remember Ed's niece, Britney? She came for Thanksgiving?"

I acknowledged that I recalled the sulky teenager with eyes only for her phone. John went on to tell me that she had turned up at Ed and Perry's place. The couple had flown to Las Vegas for the New Year's holiday, and he had gone over to feed their cat. Britney, soaked through, shivering, and in tears, was sitting on the front porch.

"I can't get any sense out of her. She must have walked from town, but I have no idea how she got there from California. I can't reach the guys. I think they must be at a show and turned their phones off. I've left messages, but I don't know what to do with her until I hear from them." He spoke in a hoarse whisper; I guessed Britney was close by. "I think something bad happened to her."

"Perhaps you should take her to the police." As I said the words, I pictured the reception a tearful teenager would get at the police department on New Year's Eve and regretted my suggestion. Britney would be taken to an interview room to sit in a metal chair bolted to the floor in front of a scarred table to wait for whatever cop drew the short straw for duty on this particular holiday. A shift dealing with drunk drivers and bar fights would leave little patience for a non-communicative adolescent.

"But you *are* the police," John protested. "Look, you know how to handle this kind of thing. It would be awkward for me to have her here, you know, overnight— not appropriate."

"You mean you want to bring her here?" I demanded, my voice rising.

"Well, you're a woman. You can get her to talk to you. You don't have plans for the evening, do you?"

Aside from his assumption I was such a social loser that I'd be home alone on New Year's Eve, I resented his attempt to push his problem off on me. I was about to tell him so when I pictured that dismal interview room again.

"Okay, bring her here. You owe me big time." At least this would break the monotony and distract me from the temptation to see in the New Year with a bottle.

I used the twenty minutes before they arrived to find blankets and a pillow for the sofa, and some clean sweatpants and top for Britney to change into. I even had an unopened three-pack of underwear for her. I knew the bathroom was spotless and ready for guests.

When I opened the door, I saw that Britney had stopped shivering and crying, but she kept her head down, letting rats' tails of wet hair obscure her face. She wore one of John's jackets, the sleeves hanging over her hands; her legs in ripped jeans stuck down like pipe stems below. She was clutching a backpack to her chest.

"Britney, this is Christine. She's the—" John stopped himself saying 'police detective,' "—friend you met at Thanksgiving. She'll look after you until your uncles get back." He spoke in a false, hearty tone, looking around the living room rather than meeting my eye.

"Hi, Britney," I said. She raised her face to stare at me but said nothing. The girl was ashy pale except where makeup had streaked into dark smudges beneath her eyes. She looked pitifully young.

"So, I'll leave you to it," said John, already backing towards the door. "Um, can I…?" He gestured at the jacket. Britney shrugged out of it, letting it drop to the floor to reveal a pink hoodie inadequate for a spring day, let alone a stormy night in December. She gripped the backpack to her again.

After John left—neither Britney nor I said goodbye to him—I stood silently for a moment, wondering what the best approach would be. I settled for calm and detached. "Anything you need right now?"

"I want to charge my phone." *Lo, she speaks*. I led her into the kitchen and showed her the charging station.

"It's not working," she whined. I worried she was about to cry again.

"If the battery's completely dead, it will take a few minutes to start charging. You can take a shower and change into some dry clothes while it charges. I've put some things in the bathroom. They'll be a bit big, but good enough for tonight."

As I showed her how the shower worked, the thought struck me that she should not be washing. If "something bad" had happened to her as John suggested—he meant sexual assault—I should take her to the emergency room where they would examine her using a rape kit to collect evidence. But I was supposed to be a friend, not a cop, and I knew, with even the most sympathetic ER nurse, the process could be harrowing. Wouldn't she have said if she'd been assaulted? Perhaps it was more important to get her trust first—and to get her warm and dry, and out of those wet clothes.

I was still enough of a cop to want a look in that all-important backpack, but Britney had taken it with her into the bathroom. I contented myself with making grilled cheese sandwiches and a pot of coffee, keeping an ear open for the water sounds.

When Britney emerged, she looked even younger than before, with her face scrubbed clean and wet hair combed back from her face. She made straight for the phone.

"It's not charging!" There was panic in her voice.

"Let me look." I took the device from her and examined it. There were some scratches on the bottom edge. I extracted my own phone and compared the weight with Britney's. "Has the phone been with you all the time?"

She glared at me. "Why won't it work?"

"I think someone's taken the battery out, or maybe the sim card."

Her mouth fell open. Before she could start bawling I said, "Let's eat, and then we'll work out what to do. What do you want to drink: coffee? OJ? Milk?"

That diverted her. She gave me a look of scorn. "Coffee, black, sugar."

Whatever had happened to Britney, her appetite was

unaffected. She devoured two sandwiches and a bag of potato chips. I poured her some water and pointed at the fruit bowl. "Grab an apple and let's go sit in the comfortable chairs."

Food had boosted her a little, but I could see she was exhausted. I wanted to get her story before she fell asleep on me. I hoped I'd given her enough time and space to open up. "When did you leave California?"

She considered the question. "Yesterday. Seems like years."

Little by little, she related what had happened since she walked out of the rehab clinic in Santa Rosa the day before. A friend she had met at the facility had offered her a ride to Portland. "Dev was going there for a job. He said there might be work for me there too."

"What about your parents? Don't they support you? Why do you need to work?"

Britney explained her parents were divorced and both had started new families. "They don't want me around, except as a babysitter. They'd rather pay the big bucks to keep me in rehab. I want to travel. I'm sick of California."

She and Dev got to Portland about nine p.m. and went to the house of the man who had promised Dev a job. "He had a really cool place. There was a media room and a sauna and the kitchen was all marble and white and shit." Britney had been left there while the men went out to introduce Dev to the people he'd be working with. She'd wandered around for a bit, then fell asleep on a sofa in the media room. Dev and his boss woke her when they returned about two a.m. "They were acting wild— really loud and laughing and shit. They were high. Anyway, they said we all had to go to Seattle—that's where the job for me was. I didn't want to go. For starters, I didn't want to get in a car with them high like that. It was the middle of the night, I just wanted to sleep. It was all fucked up."

Somehow, the three of them made it up I-5 without crashing or being pulled over by the highway patrol. "They took me to this house—well, rooms over a shop, a nail salon, I think. It was getting light by then. The place looked sketchy. I told Dev I didn't want to go inside, that I'd just call my uncles and get them to pick me up. Dev got mad at me—that's when he grabbed my phone. Anyway, the boss guy and Dev went off and talked a bit, and then Dev told me, okay, just go upstairs, call your uncles and wait there. They had some business to see to, so they left."

I could see that Britney was getting to the hardest part of the story. She fidgeted, picking at a nail, and glancing around the room nervously. "What's that?" She nodded at Victoria.

"It's a copy of a statue from Greece." I didn't think Britney would be interested in a lecture on ancient Cycladic culture. "John gave it to me for Christmas."

"Weird," was her comment. I looked at the statue with a new perception. The four-thousand-year-old model, a girl on the cusp of womanhood, prepared for ritual sacrifice, was more Britney than Victoria.

"What happened then?" I prompted.

"There were three girls in the apartment over the shop. Asian. Two of them were asleep or passed out. They were wearing bras and pants, nothing else. The one that was awake didn't speak English. She followed me around, hanging on me, screeching in this foreign language. I tried my phone—it was dead. Thought it was just the battery, but I bet Dev fucked with it before he went. I tried to leave—the door was locked from the outside. And this girl right next to me all the time, even when I said I needed to go to the bathroom. In the end, I just pushed her down and ran in there. I wedged the door handle." Britney's eyes were squeezed shut and her hands clenched. "There were needles on the sink. I don't do needles—ever. I do pills—*did* pills, booze, pot. Never needles. That's when I guessed what the place was and what they wanted: drug me up and keep me there. The bathroom window was high up in the wall. I could hear that girl outside the door screaming at me. I climbed up on the john and pushed myself through. I dropped maybe twelve feet, but I landed okay. Then I ran."

She stopped speaking, panting a little with the effort of reliving the experience.

"You were brave." My own tears were close. Britney was so young. Stupid maybe, but she had no one to guide her. I was the same age when my parents died. I could so easily have drifted into drugs, homelessness, prostitution. I'd found a hard center inside me: an instinct for self-preservation, and it drove me forward. I thought Britney had found that same instinct.

She told the rest of the story quickly. Knowing every downhill in Seattle leads to the waterfront, she found her way to Pike Street Market and talked her way onto a tour bus full of senior citizens headed for the Indian casinos. She remembered there was a casino at the I-5 exit for Ed and Perry's house. By the time the bus reached the casino, Britney was everyone's substitute granddaughter. They fed her candy and posed for selfies with her. She walked the last four miles through the freezing rain.

She fell asleep on my sofa like a baby, mouth slightly open, cheek cradled on her hands. I tucked the blanket around her, resisting the urge to bend and kiss her head. Tomorrow I'd become a cop again. I'd plumb for details: the name of the bastard with the fancy house in Portland, addresses and landmarks that I could pass on to local police. For now, I was content to sit watching Britney sleep, feeling an ache in my chest that I had a nasty suspicion might be maternal instinct. I told myself to get a grip.

Before I went to my own bedroom, I gently eased open the zip on Britney's backpack. Inside, besides a wallet and a make-up pouch, were several notebooks. I extracted one and looked inside just long enough to see it was a journal, every page covered in round childish handwriting. I replaced the notebook without reading it.

Chapter 31

New Year's Day: another damn holiday when nothing gets done. The world sleeps in and spends the rest of the day nursing a hangover in front of a football game on TV.

Not me. I was up with the lark, thanks to a phone call from John telling me Ed and Perry had finally picked up their messages at four a.m. and headed for the airport. Their flight from Vegas was scheduled to land in Seattle at 9:40 a.m.

Britney—lucky thing—slept through the phone's ring. We ate our scrambled eggs together later, neither of us speaking more than monosyllables. Without a phone to hunch over and scroll, Britney appeared disoriented, aimless. To engage her, I suggested she try to reconstruct the location of the place where she'd been imprisoned. I summoned up a street map of Seattle on my computer screen and zoomed out from Pike Street Market. Britney wasn't great at map-reading, but with the help of the street view app and my own sketchy knowledge of Emerald City neighborhoods, we were able to make a good stab at the address. We were not so fortunate placing the mansion in Portland, however.

"Can you remember the name of the man Dev took you to?" I asked.

"Dev just called him 'Chef'—you know, like a cook in a restaurant. I don't think he was a chef though."

"What about Dev's last name?"

"Oh, he's just Dev." She tossed her hair and gave me a sideways look that implied I was hopelessly uncool to suggest he should have a last name, or that she should know it.

"Hmm." Dev would probably be traceable through his residence at the rehab facility where he'd met Britney. "Is there anything else you can remember about 'Chef'?"

She huffed a bit, as if it was an imposition to have to think about this. "So, he was old—older than you, maybe forty? And he talked weird."

"You mean he had an accent?"

"I guess…I mean he spoke English okay, just didn't open his mouth very wide. Maybe he had bad teeth." She let out a cackle. The well of sympathy I'd felt for Brittany the previous evening was running dry. I probed for more details from various angles but got nowhere.

She dressed in her own clothes which I had washed and dried, then disappeared into the bathroom for fifteen minutes to apply makeup. When she emerged, she was again the sulky teenager I had met at Thanksgiving. In a way, I was pleased: she demonstrated the resiliency of youth. Twenty-four hours after barely escaping from being trafficked into prostitution, the sneer was as firmly in place as her black eyeliner and nose ring.

Ed dropped Perry at their place before arriving at the apartment to pick Britney up. When I buzzed him in, he looked haggard: New Year's Eve partying and a night without sleep, I thought. When he folded Britney into a long, close hug, I realized that anxiety about his niece played a part too. Initially, Britney stiffened away, but after a couple of seconds, she relaxed against him. I tactfully left them to go make more coffee, although I could overhear their conversation.

"I spoke to your mom—" Ed began.

"I'm not going to her place!" Britney shrilled.

"That's not—"

"Or back to that rehab clinic. They just tell you the same stuff over and over. It's boring!"

"You're not going back to rehab, not that overpriced holding pen anyway. Wait!" Ed held a hand up as Britney was about to launch into another objection. "I agree you don't need more rehab, and you and your mother would kill each other living in the same house. I'm suggesting you stay with Perry and me, but if that's going to work for more than a couple of weeks, we have to reach some agreements." He paused to make sure she was listening. "First of all, you need to be back in school—hey, don't make that face. Before you dropped out, you were getting good grades, involved in activities, sports. You have a chance at a fresh start here. Classes start up again on Tuesday, and I'd like you to be there."

I slipped a tray onto the coffee table and then hovered at the side of the room. Britney looked miserable, head down, fiddling with the drawstring on her hoodie. Ed kept his hand on her shoulder.

"I won't know anyone. They'll hate me."

"I know it will be hard, starting something always is, but this is your chance, Britney. You can be a new person, do new things, make new friends, have a new life."

"You going to drug test me?" Her tone was belligerent.

"Do we need to?" Ed smiled.

I could see the girl was struggling to trust her uncle,

and to trust herself. She'd spent time and energy developing a defiant shell and reacting to perceived grievances. How could she believe that if circumstances were different, she could be different too?

"All my things are in Santa Rosa," she mumbled. "I don't have any clothes—or a phone."

"Well, I'll see about adding you to our phone plan once you start school. We can talk about that." Ed turned to me. "Christine, any chance you'd have some time before Tuesday to take Britney shopping for essentials?"

I would rather have my leg amputated without anesthetic than go clothes shopping with a teenager. "Sure, I've got some time."

"Great!"

****

I spent the rest of my New Year's Day, after Ed took Britney home, being a good citizen. I went through my contacts in the Seattle and Portland police departments to identify officers in the vice squad. Of course, being a holiday, no one picked up my calls, but I left a few detailed voicemails pointing them at possible drug and human trafficking operations. I hoped that good intentions for the New Year might motivate them to follow up. I also dug out the number of a former local cop who now worked for the school district doing security training: a thankless job, anticipating bomb threats and organizing active shooter drills. With luck, he hadn't heard about my enforced medical leave.

"Jay, a couple of sources told me about two guys dealing drugs or recruiting dealers at the high schools." I gave him the names of the two schools Franco Gutierrez and Colin Devry attended, as well as a description of the car mentioned.

"Is this connected with the fentanyl deaths? The Joint Drug Task Force you're working on?" In spite of being woken from a nap, Jay was on the ball. "Terrible thing about that kid just before Christmas."

"Uh-huh. I've been looking into some cold cases that might be related and came across these tips. I thought you'd want to keep an eye out when classes start on Tuesday."

"Thanks, Christine—I certainly will."

I flipped through the rest of the closed files I had slid into my backpack on that last day at the Department but found nothing new to snag my attention. I remembered I'd sent some phones in the corresponding evidence boxes away for analysis and wondered if anything had come back yet. Perhaps the tech guys had ignored my request, now that I was no longer on active duty. Picturing those boxes lined up in the dark of the basement, I felt a pang of longing for my old job. If I could just creep into the squad room and log onto a terminal, I'd be able to roam through reports at will, review video footage, pursue connections, and push coworkers for follow-up. But instead, I was confined to incomplete paper records, dependent on the casual cooperation of the few colleagues who might talk to me, and unable to even conduct an interview without subterfuge.

I had to get back on the job. I'd never been inactive for so long. The apartment was beginning to feel like a prison. Humiliating as the idea was, I decided to plead with Kleinberg for a date for a fitness-for-duty exam. He'd probably refuse or impose unreasonable conditions. What if he insisted I seek counseling before he'd agree to schedule the exam? I'd do it—whatever it took. I didn't need therapy; I'd proved to myself I could handle my drinking problem on my own—no Alcoholics Anonymous meetings for me. And I knew how to bluff my way through one-on-one counseling sessions. I hoped he'd give me the chance before I really went insane.

Chapter 32

John returned to work on the second day of the year, determined to fill in the gaps he now recognized in the autopsy reports completed in the earlier months of his tenure as Medical Examiner. However, during his absence over the holidays, five bodies had been checked into the refrigerated steel lockers that lined the examination room, the cause of death to be determined. He rephrased his New Year's Resolution in prospective terms: he would carry out these upcoming autopsies with meticulous care, keeping his mind open to all possibilities. He would review the scene of death, interview the first responders, question all assumptions. The closed cases would have to wait.

"Who secured the scene?" John asked as the first body was wheeled over to the examination table.

His assistant was a mousey woman in her twenties, adept at routine forensic testing of blood, semen, saliva, and other bodily fluids, but uninterested in the bigger picture. Unprepared for her boss's new approach, she stared at him, open-mouthed. "I don't know, Dr. Williams. The intake form just says the body was transported by…" she consulted a computer screen, "County Ambulance Unit 23. The EMTs' names are here, but there doesn't appear to be any PD officer assigned."

"Well, find out. The police must have been called.

A body in a car is a suspicious death; it needs investigation."

"No signs of violence," the assistant read sulkily from the screen. *What's got into him?* "Probably ODed."

"Exactly!" John raised his voice, and the young woman shrank further. "We have a fentanyl epidemic on our hands! How are we going to control it unless every case is thoroughly analyzed from start to finish!"

By lunchtime, John had completed the autopsy. Although lab results would take longer, there was every sign that cause of death was a drug overdose, probably fentanyl. He tracked down the patrol officer who had been at the scene of death.

"Yeah, I phoned it in to the detective squad. Detective Myers arranged for the car to be impounded. He said he'd handle it from there. I expect he'll be calling you."

Why hadn't Myers called the M.E.'s office already? John was about to grab the handset when he remembered the voicemail he'd received from Myers a couple of days before about Victoria Hartman. John had returned the call and left a message telling him when he'd be back in the office. Then all the bother of Britney turning up and getting Ed and Perry home had driven Myers' call out of his mind.

His assistant stuck her head in the door, nervous about penetrating further into the office after the boss's earlier outburst. "There's a Detective Myers been waiting to see you. Do you have time to talk to him now?"

"Yes! Send him up." Good. He could discuss Victoria Hartman's possible murder as well as get the context for the new drug death.

Myers was younger than John expected. He wore a winter jacket with wide shoulders that exaggerated his build. He shrugged it off to reveal a preppy uniform of button-down shirt and khaki pants—a nineteen-fifties college boy, except for the shoulder holster. Seeming nervous, he launched straight into an explanation for his visit.

"I came across some video we were reviewing as part of another inquiry. I think, um, we maybe missed something first time around with the Victoria Hartman case."

John raised his eyebrows, but kept quiet, waiting to see what Myers had found out.

"It wasn't my case," Myers rushed on. "The detective who handled it is on leave, so…"

So you're going to throw Christine under the bus, John thought. Time to intervene. "Yes, Detective Sergeant McQuarry spoke to me several times about her hunch that the death was suspicious, and I've reviewed the autopsy report carefully. What does the video show?"

Myers gulped. His plan to claim sole credit for uncovering a murder was falling apart. He hadn't guessed that Christine and the M.E. were in close contact. "Yeah, so Hartman shows up as a guest at an airport hotel the day before she turns up dead, but she wasn't alone. It looks like she was meeting a boy there— young enough to be her son. Their meeting is caught on the hotel reception video feed. She'd reserved a separate room for him."

"And she didn't look suicidal?"

"No. There's more. The next evening there's an altercation in the lobby. This boy gets into it with an older man. The man drags the kid out of the hotel. It's all on the video, time shown, six-ten p.m. Hartman's not there. She never shows up in the lobby again. Here's the thing: she booked two rooms for three days but she checks out of both later that night. Does it online, via the app on the room TV. None of the hotel staff see or talk to her. Weird, huh?"

"Hmm. What puzzles me, Detective Myers, is why you bring this to me and not to Captain Kleinberg."

Myers reddened, fumbling for a response. "I, er, wanted to run it past you first, in case there was anything new you'd found, you know, after the autopsy. The captain doesn't like to reopen old cases." He gave a half-laugh. "He says we have enough new ones to solve."

John surmised the real reason was that Myers hoped John would approach Kleinberg and take the initial heat for reopening the file based on his inadequate autopsy report. "Have you identified the man who abducted the boy?"

"Not yet, but I've got a lead. So my theory is, he's the dad and he doesn't want his son consorting with Hartman for whatever reason, which gives him a motive to kill her, don't ya think?"

John was beginning to actively dislike Myers. Christine's assessment that he was dumb but ambitious was at least half right. "Well, here's what I'd advise. Share all this information with Christine McQuarry. She knows a lot more about the whole background than you do. She may be on inactive status, but she's not incapacitated. She'll tell you what the next steps are. And when the two of you are ready to take it to Captain Kleinberg, I'll be happy to come along and explain why some of the autopsy findings point to a finding of homicide."

As soon as Myers left the office, John called Christine.

Chapter 33

I phoned Kleinberg, ready to humiliate myself, but he didn't pick up, and I wasn't going to leave a voicemail that he could misinterpret or ignore. Ed was dropping Britney off for the shopping expedition at eleven, so I put the files away and prepared myself for retail torture.

I hate the mall. At least Britney knew exactly which stores she wanted to go to, so I was spared a soul-destroying meander through the post-holiday crowds fighting to return or exchange gifts. However, she seemed determined to examine every item on the racks. Trying to accelerate the process, I proffered a couple of cute sweaters. The curled lip of disdain I received in return drove me to the front of the store where I stationed myself and Ed's credit card next to the cashier. While I waited, I surveyed the packs of teens cruising the common areas. The girls wore too much eye makeup, and jeans so ripped it was a wonder they held together. They clung onto each other, talking loud and laughing, while casting slant eyes at the boys that hung out in separate groups. I had missed out on these kinds of teenage rituals, and now I regarded them with distaste. God, I was getting old!

Britney arrived with an armful of clothes. Following Ed's instructions, I vetted the pile and rejected a sparkly crop top and a micro-length skirt. "It's the Pacific Northwest, Britney, not California. You'd die of cold." I pointed out the plate glass window at her peer group's standard uniform. "Jeans and hoodies, maybe leggings and an oversized flannel shirt—you'll want to blend in on your first day."

After some haggling, we settled on several items and moved on to shoes. I was paying for a pair of high-top sneakers when my phone rang. John. I wasn't in the mood to hear more of his self-recrimination, so I declined the call. He could leave a voicemail. Another call came in as we were walking across the parking lot. This one I accepted.

"Hi, James. Any response from the Lemesurs yet?"

"No, nothing." This time James Anderson wasted no time on niceties. He sounded concerned. "It's been three days since my letter was delivered. I asked Gaston to call immediately. I think I'll have to retain an investigator in Vancouver to follow up."

"I'll go." I'd offered before, but James had turned me down: before his formal letter was delivered it would have been premature.

"But this is a civil matter, not police business. Won't you get into trouble with the police department?"

No more trouble than I'm in at present, I thought. Time to come clean. "Actually, I'm on leave at present…medical leave."

A long pause, and then, "Oh?"

"Yeah. A misunderstanding, really. I'm waiting for an appointment for my fit-for-duty exam, but right now my time's my own. If you give me the Lemesurs' address, I'll check it out and report back. I can do it today."

Britney was exhaling dramatically, tired of waiting for me to unlock the car. I clicked it open and we got in.

Anderson was still making up his mind.

"Well, all right. But don't approach them without talking to me first. Here's the address." I entered the information into my phone, and we said our goodbyes.

"What are you smiling at?" Britney asked as we reversed out of the parking spot.

I dropped Britney off at Ed and Perry's place, then hot-footed it back to my apartment. At last things were moving, and I was jazzed. I filled my backpack with power bars and water bottles, a reversible jacket and baseball cap in case I needed a quick change of look. Stakeouts could be boring, but I was looking forward to this one. I thought James would just want me to verify the address and who lived there, but I was prepared for anything. I grabbed my passport and headed out.

I was in line at the border when I remembered John's call. He had left me a voicemail, but just then the line moved forward. I switched my phone to airplane mode: my stingy phone plan doesn't cover service in Canada, and I didn't want distractions anyway.

Nothing to declare and forty minutes later I was searching for the turn off, No. 4 Road in Richmond, that would lead to Chestnut Close, the housing development where Gaston and his father lived. Chestnut Close turned out to be parallel rows of townhouses, garage on ground floor front and two levels of living accommodation above. I parked a few doors down from my target, number fifteen, and assessed the street. At four p.m. it was getting dark, but few lights shone from the houses. The residents were probably still at work. I watched a kid on a bike circle around the end of the row. Otherwise there was no traffic.

After a few minutes, I left the car and followed in

the biker's tracks around to the back of the homes. Each had a low-walled courtyard accessed by a back door. Some of the courtyards were tastefully arranged with evergreens in large ceramic plant pots, wrought iron café tables and chairs. The courtyard behind number fifteen contained only a trash can and some cardboard boxes. I saw the kid from earlier working on his bike behind number nineteen. I sauntered up to him.

"Nice wheels. What's the problem?" I asked, hoping I sounded as if I knew something about bicycle maintenance.

"Suspension's screwed up. Might have to take it to the shop." The boy was about fifteen, pleasant-faced and polite. He'd be a good influence on Britney.

"Hmm." I didn't know bikes even had suspensions. Time to change the subject. "Do you know a kid called Gaston Lemesur?"

"Sure. He lives a couple of doors down." He indicated with a lift of his chin. "But I haven't seen him recently."

"Away for the holidays?"

"No, he's been gone longer than that. He goes to my school, a couple of years ahead of me, but I haven't seen him there for months."

"Maybe the family moved," I suggested.

"Don't think so. I haven't seen a moving van or a For Sale sign, and I'm pretty sure I've seen his dad's car around. It's a Beemer."

"Okay, thanks. Good luck with the suspension." I turned and walked nonchalantly past the Lemesur house. It was completely dark now and lights shone from several windows along the row, but not from the Lemesur house. I went back around to my car at the front.

I ate a power bar and drank some water. In the next thirty minutes, a couple of garage doors swung open remotely and returning residents pulled in. A few more lights turned on. Two men wearing baseball caps, hunched into puffy jackets, came along the sidewalk towards and past my car. I contemplated eating another power bar.

Out of nowhere, I heard the sound of my rear drivers-side door opening. Before I could turn, an arm snaked around my neck and jerked my head back, cutting off my breathing. I scrabbled ineffectively at the imprisoning arm. The passenger side door opened, and I saw out of the corner of my eye one of the puffy jacketed men climb in. Something hard poked into my side.

"What you playing at?" The voice was low and gruff, a trace of an accent.

I made some strangled sounds in response. The pain in my throat was intense. My brain raced: who were these men and what did they want? Jean-Paul Lemesur's criminal contacts? Lemesur himself? Random carjackers? How had I been so stupid as to leave the doors unlocked?

"Stop struggling. I got a gun on you. If you quiet down, my guy will let you breathe."

I lowered my hands, and the arm loosened a tad. I drew a ragged breath. "Who are you?" I croaked.

"Uh-uh. I ask the questions."

Without letting go of his hold on me, the man in the back seat passed my backpack forward. The guy with the gun awkwardly groped around inside it and extracted my passport. The pressure of the gun barrel in my ribs did not vary.

"Christine McQuarry, American." He leaned toward

me, close enough that I could feel his breath, but I still couldn't turn my head to get a good look at him. "So, I'm gonna ask you again—what you playing at?"

Chapter 34

Except for that brief moment of panic when I couldn't breathe, I wasn't scared. That's not bravado—I just switched into cop mode. I'd been trained for kidnappings and hostage situations: make an assessment and look for opportunities—as in, what mistakes is the perpetrator making? My assessment: the man in the passenger seat was in charge. The guy in the back didn't speak; he followed instructions. The arm around my neck prevented me from getting a straight-on look at the boss, but from what I'd noticed when the two approached on the sidewalk, he was probably in his forties, and although the baseball cap was pulled down, I had the impression he was dark-haired. There was the trace of an accent I couldn't place: could it be French-Canadian?

There was no such thing as a perfect crime, especially an opportunistic attack like this one. I had already identified one mistake, an unnecessary one. If these guys wanted to know why I was sitting in a parked car on an ordinary residential street, they could have tapped politely on the window and asked whether they could be of help. Instead, they'd gone nuclear, escalating the encounter into violence. Why the hair trigger? Something to work out later. Right now, I would give them exactly the same information I would have given if they had taken the low-key approach.

"I'm helping out a lawyer located in Philadelphia.

He's handling the estate of a woman who died recently. One of the beneficiaries in her will lives on this street. The lawyer's had no reply to his letter so he asked me to check out the address." I kept my voice level and my eyes forward. "Look, could you stop throttling me? I'm not trying to escape."

The man with the gun nodded to his colleague and the arm was withdrawn. I massaged my neck, turning my head side to side, and getting a good fix on my assailant. I'd bet money it was Gaston's father, but I wouldn't know for sure until I could get hold of the RCMP's mug shot.

"Why not knock on zuh door like a normal person?" Again, the accent.

"No lights on, nobody home. I was waiting until someone arrived."

A pause. Then, "So what's dis *benny-fishy-ree* get?"

I turned towards him. There was a distinctly avaricious gleam in the man's eye: Bingo! He was hooked. "I believe the entire estate."

"How much?"

"I don't know exactly."

The gun jabbed into my ribs. "Take a guess," he snarled.

I pretended to hesitate. The gun barrel twisted. "I, er, think it might be several million." There was an intake of breath from the back seat, and Lemesur (if it *was* him) threw a dirty glance in that direction. "But obviously, the lawyer has to be absolutely satisfied that he's got the right person," I continued. "The money won't be handed over without the beneficiary providing proof of his—or her—identity."

"Obviously." Lemesur mimicked my officious tone.

"Okay, start driving."

"What?"

"You deaf? I said, drive!"

I turned on the engine and pulled away from the curb. Lemesur barked out directions, forcing me to make a series of left and right turns that quickly had me disoriented. We left the residential neighborhood and without passing any landmarks I could recognize, we plunged into a grim area of industrial buildings and warehouses. It was now close to seven p.m. and we saw few cars and no pedestrians. Except for security lights on the corners of the buildings, the surroundings were dark. After more confusing turns that finished in a dead end with a high brick wall, I was told to stop.

"Get out and go face de wall."

"Why? Are you going to shoot me?" I was almost certain they wouldn't.

"Don' tempt me." He reached across and opened my door, pushing me so hard I almost fell out of the car. I scrambled to exit before he could push me again.

"My phone? I don't know where I am!"

He laughed. The man in the back got out and took the driver's seat. I had a good look at his face for the first time. About the same age as Lemesur, with several days of stubble, and a spider tattoo on his neck. The car reversed out of the cul de sac at speed. I ran after it, only to see taillights disappearing around a corner. I continued running but by the time I reached the corner the car had disappeared.

It took me half an hour to work my way out of the maze of empty buildings and neglected industrial lots to something resembling civilization. By then I was limping from a stumble into a pothole, my palms grazed from the fall. The lights of a commercial district led me forward to a car dealer's lot. I threaded my way between new SUVs toward the brightly lit showroom. I was just in time: a man with keys in his hand was waiting for a woman to precede him through the showroom door.

"Excuse me!" I called. "Can you help me? I've been carjacked."

"Oh, no, that's terrible. Come inside," the man answered. "We were just closing up."

Seeing my disheveled state, the woman said, "Let me get you a glass of water."

I could have wept at their kindness. The adrenaline that had driven me forward through the dark streets ebbed away. I sank onto the bench the woman indicated and took some deep breaths.

"Have you called the police?"

"They have my phone, my wallet—everything!"

"Here, you can use my phone." Canadians are so polite—most of them. The man handed his device to me at the same moment his colleague proffered a glass of water. I sipped from the glass, considering the phone in my other hand. I should call the police. That was what an ordinary crime victim would do. But I was police myself, and I knew the process these things followed. I would be taken to an office and asked endless questions. I wouldn't get home tonight. Plus, if I gave them Lemesur's name and address, they would totally screw up the scheme I was hatching to find Gaston. Now that I had dangled the prospect of millions of dollars in front of Lemesur, I was pretty sure he'd break cover and come to the States with Gaston to claim the inheritance. If he was being investigated for carjacking and kidnapping, he'd find a way to disappear again with his son.

"Would you like me to make the call?" The car salesman thought I was suffering from shock. He extended his hand for the device.

"No, it's all right. I'll call. I just need some fresh air." I took the phone outside, trying to remember John's number. I had it stored in my contacts, but could only vaguely recall the digits. I'd get him to come and collect me, and send these nice folks home while I waited. In the meantime, I'd think about the problem of how to cross the border without a passport. What *was* his number?

I was gazing around, searching my brain, when my eye rested on something out of place at the far corner of the lot. Next to the shiny new Japanese models sat a shabby-looking wagon. I turned back to my saviors.

"That car?" I pointed. "Is it…? Where did it…?"

"Huh! I'm not sure what it's doing there. Not one of ours." The man turned to his colleague who was also staring at the misfit vehicle.

"It wasn't here earlier. I was showing a vehicle on that row about an hour ago. Someone must have parked it after dark."

I was already ten yards away. "It's mine!" I ran down the line of new cars, the other two following. The car was unlocked. I pulled the driver's door open, then looked at the salespeople. They were staring at me with suspicion. I could see the thought cross their faces: was this some kind of scam?

"No, really—this is my car. And look, my wallet and passport and everything." I gestured to the mess of my belongings scattered in the well on the passenger side. "My name is Christine McQuarry. Please—go and check."

Still frowning, the man went around to the other side

of the car, opened the door and picked up my passport. "Yes, that's the name." He gathered up my phone and wallet and brought them to me. "Well, I guess you can report it on your phone now."

I gave him his own device back. "I'm so grateful. You've both been very kind. I won't keep you hanging around in the cold any longer." Still burbling my thanks, I climbed into the car and started the engine. "Oh, one more thing—can you direct me to 99 South?"

It seemed to take no time at all to find my way back to the highway and reach the U.S. border. Just a few cars ahead of me in line. I felt ebullient. Yes, things had looked sketchy for a moment, but the end result was that I had baited a trap that might lure Victoria's killer back into my jurisdiction. While I waited, I flicked the phone off airplane mode. Immediately, incoming notifications pinged and buzzed. I remembered I'd never listened to John's voicemail from lunchtime. The line moved forward. I decided to pull over and check messages as soon as I was back stateside.

"Did you buy anything in Canada?"

"No!" I couldn't help giving the border officer a big grin.

He glowered back and said, "Welcome home," and waved me through. I took the first exit and found a place to park. Time to catch up with what had been happening at home while I was in foreign parts.

The most recent message was a text from John: "*Answer your phone! I'm worried about you!*" I felt a rush of warm feeling. He really cared about me! Almost at once, the warmth was replaced by irritation. John didn't own me. Why should answering his calls be my number one priority?

The next two notifications were voicemails. I didn't recognize one of the numbers, but the other came from Myers. I hoped he'd completed his review of the lobby security video and had some news for me.

"Hey. So I asked the RCMP for info on a guy in the lobby video." Myers sounded sheepish and a little resentful. *"You're gonna get a call. Seems we—you!— stirred up a hornet's nest. There's a task force meeting tomorrow morning. Don't fuck this up."*

Nice. Myers was, as usual, looking after number one. He'd made an identification but wasn't going to confirm to me that it was Gaston or Jean-Paul Lemesur. I guessed he'd tried to claim the glory for himself but that plan had gone south, and now the Canadians wanted to talk to me, the source. Was I invited to this meeting? Where and when was it? Myers hadn't given me the essential information, probably to make me look bad if I didn't show up. Perhaps the unknown caller could shed some light.

"Hello, Sergeant McQuarry? This is Chief Superintendent Kenneth Henderson of the Royal Canadian Mounted Police in B.C. I'm the senior Canadian representative on the joint drug task force." I was impressed by his rank, and the clipped, almost British accent which suggested a man who didn't suffer fools gladly. I wondered if he was the one who had cut Myers down to size. I liked the Canadian cop already. *"I understand that you are pursuing an inquiry into a suspicious death in your jurisdiction and require confirmation of the identity of a suspect caught on video."* Hmm, the most I'd realistically hoped for from the video was evidence that Gaston had met up with Victoria at the hotel. When I'd crossed into Canada that

morning, my theory that his father Jean-Paul had killed Victoria was only that—a theory. Now it seemed the father might have been caught on video as well, *and* he was a person of interest to the Canadian police. Henderson continued, "*I'd like to meet you at your office tomorrow at nine a.m. I've notified your Captain*—" I could hear the shuffling of papers in the background of the recording—"*Kleinberg, and I believe the other detective*—" more shuffling—"*Myers and the Medical Examiner will also be present. In the meantime, I must warn you not to take any action that might alert Lemesur to your investigation. I hope that's understood.*"

Oops. Staking out Lemesur's home, and then spending an hour at gunpoint with him in my car was not going to please the Chief Superintendent. I wondered if I could risk not telling anyone about today's adventure. Lemesur knew my name and nationality, what I looked like and what car I drove. It wouldn't be hard for him to find out I was a cop. Except I wasn't a cop at present—I was serving an indefinite suspension. I didn't think Henderson knew that yet, but as soon as he walked into Kleinberg's office tomorrow, he'd find out. This was getting complicated.

I put the problem aside to listen to the voicemail John had left earlier and I had ignored all day. Once I heard him describe the video that Myers had shown him, things began to make sense. The day before Victoria's body was found, a young man—Gaston Lemesur—met her in the hotel lobby. My belief that mother and son were at last reunited—even if only a day before Victoria's death—was vindicated. The next day, an altercation took place in the lobby between the same boy and an older man, identified now by the RCMP as Jean-

Paul Lemesur. He had dragged his son out of the hotel just a few hours before Victoria was found dead in a downtown doorway.

"*So you were right all along*," concluded John's voicemail. "*Myers and I are taking this new evidence plus my revised autopsy report to Captain Kleinberg tomorrow. We're going to get you reinstated and the case reopened.*"

If only it were that simple. There were the other small matters of impersonating a police officer, getting involved in a drunken brawl, and stealing police files. Kleinberg was unlikely to change his mind about my suspension. I turned on the engine and pulled out into southbound traffic. Perhaps things would look simpler after a good night's sleep.

Chapter 35

I dressed in my best business casual for the meeting: the blazer and dark pants I'd worn to interview Justine Norman's sister Jessica—was that really less than a week ago? Thinking of Jessica and her dead sister brought Frank Gutierrez to mind. School would be back in session now after the winter break, and I had a lead to follow up—"white guys in nice cars"—which might steer me to who killed Marta Gutierrez and dressed it up as a fentanyl overdose. Right now, I needed to prioritize Victoria Hartman, but after this morning's session I promised myself I'd make a to-do list. Whether or not I was reinstated to the department, I owed it to the families to get to the truth. The police department was too ready to ascribe every drug death to some accidental overdose. I had been as guilty as the rest of making easy assumptions…until I'd seen my own face staring up at me from a mortuary table. My doppelgänger had driven me crazy for a while, but ultimately she'd given me a purpose.

Another item on the to-do list was a report to James Anderson. With his rigid standards of professional conduct, the elderly attorney would be disturbed to hear about my encounter with Lemesur and his sidekick. Anderson had been very clear that I shouldn't talk to either father or son. Maybe he'd be soothed by the news that I'd baited the trap that would get them to contact him.

I'd texted John asking to meet outside the police department so we could go in together. I wanted someone with me when I entered Kleinberg's office, in case he tried to bar me from attending the meeting. John took my request as evidence I'd now forgiven him for throwing me under the bus in the first place and was happy to agree. I hadn't forgiven him—not completely—but I needed all the allies I could get.

With eyes fixed ahead, I strode through the squad room, John behind me. I could almost hear the heads swiveling to stare at us. I rapped on Kleinberg's office door.

"Come!" came the familiar bark from inside.

Although the captain sat behind his over-large and empty desk, the commanding presence in the room was in the visitor's chair across from him. Chief Superintendent Kenneth Henderson rose to his feet and turned to greet us. He was in his fifties, roughly the same age as Kleinberg, but a head taller and forty pounds slimmer. Although he was wearing a business suit with an open-neck shirt beneath, his military bearing suggested he was wearing a uniform, emphasized by his clean-shaven face and close-cropped gray hair. He gave a tight-lipped smile as he extended his hand.

"Detective Sergeant McQuarry? Pleased to meet you. And you are?" Henderson turned to John. I was amused to see John's discomfiture at being, for once, the "plus one."

"John Williams, Medical Examiner. I've brought some updated autopsy findings that might be helpful."

"Oh?" Henderson didn't seem interested. "Detective Myers, would you mind fetching two more chairs?" I hadn't noticed Myers sitting in the corner until then. He was hunched into his jacket, trying to be invisible. He stumbled past us to do the senior officer's bidding.

Kleinberg let out a forceful breath. "Well, I didn't realize this was going to be a mass assembly. On the phone, you just mentioned a drug task force update." Changing his tone from breezy to accusatory, he turned to me. "McQuarry, what are you doing here? You're no longer on the task force."

Before I could respond, Henderson cut in. "I invited her, Captain. She's made some connections that might link us to the top man in the fentanyl smuggling operation, someone whom we have been trying to catch for some time."

"But—" Kleinberg was turning red. The next words out of his mouth would reveal my disgraceful suspension. Fortunately, Myers returned at that moment with two folding chairs that he noisily deployed before retreating to his corner.

Henderson continued, "As you may know, Sergeant McQuarry has been gathering evidence regarding the possible murder last October of a woman, now identified as Victoria Hartman. Her investigation revealed a link between Ms. Hartman and a Canadian family named Lemesur."

While Henderson spoke, Kleinberg was stabbing angrily at his computer keyboard. He now waved a hand at Myers. "That case is closed. Right, Myers? Suicide?"

Myers hauled himself into a more upright sitting position. "Um, well, initially I think it was ruled an accidental overdose or suicide, but the file—"

...is missing: hidden in my apartment with the seven other files I stole. This time, John intervened to save me.

"I did the autopsy. Yes, at first I determined the overdose that caused Victoria's death was either accidental or suicide, but when Christine drew my attention to some other factors, I reassessed my findings." He proffered a folder to Henderson while Kleinberg made exasperated noises.

"And it was at that point, I believe, that you asked Detective Myers to check the lobby video recordings at the airport hotel?" Henderson invited me speak. Myers shuffled in his seat, Kleinberg glared, and I cleared my throat.

"Yes. A routine canvas of the airport hotels in connection with the task force investigation turned up a witness at that hotel who identified Victoria Hartman as a guest immediately before her death." I used my courtroom voice, expressionless and factual.

"Indeed!" Henderson turned to Myers. "So you then sought our confirmation that the man in the video was Jean-Paul Lemesur?" Myers nodded, and Henderson rotated back to me. "Perhaps you should explain how you came to connect the dead woman to Lemesur."

"In my background research on Victoria Hartman, I discovered that she had given up a baby for adoption to a family in Montreal called Lemesur. I believe she was trying to reconnect with her son when she was killed. I'm in touch with James Anderson, Victoria's attorney and the executor of her estate. She left everything to her son. Anderson traced Gaston and his father to Vancouver."

Kleinberg had clasped his hands on the desk so tightly that the knuckles showed white. He could restrain himself no longer. "Why didn't you fill me in on this?" he demanded through gritted teeth.

I widened my eyes and looked back at him blandly.

"But, sir, you remember I was placed on medical leave before Christmas. You told me to stay home."

Henderson continued as if he hadn't heard the exchange between me and the captain. "This presents a unique opportunity. We are convinced that Jean-Paul Lemesur is the top man in the fentanyl smuggling ring operating between B.C. and the U.S. But he has been careful never to personally handle the drugs or come south of the border to oversee operations. He uses middlemen, cut-offs that insulate him. The task force has caught lower-level traffickers and distributors, but no one who can implicate Lemesur."

My jaw nearly dropped. The day before, I was held at gunpoint by the head of a fentanyl operation that had caused a drug epidemic throughout the Northwest and mobilized law enforcement in two countries. I still thought Jean-Paul was an idiot for overreacting to my stake-out of his home, but I was glad I didn't know then what a dangerous idiot he was. Just then, my phone rang.

"Shut that damn thing off!" Kleinberg yelled.

I fished it out of my pocket and checked the screen. "It's James Anderson, the attorney."

"How opportune," Henderson gave another thin-lipped smile. "Perhaps you might put him on speaker."

James was probably calling to see how I'd got on in Canada. As soon as I accepted the call, I warned him, "Hi, James. You're on speaker. I'm in a meeting with members of the drug task force. They're interested in Jean-Paul Lemesur."

"Oh?" James sounded understandably confused. "Well, maybe you can call me back later. I just wanted—"

"Yes, I know, but Chief Superintendent Henderson

of the RCMP would like a word."

Henderson cleared his throat and leaned over the phone, which I placed on the desk in front of him. "Good morning, Mr. Anderson. I think you might be able to help us catch a serious criminal. Have you had any communication with Lemesur about the legacy to his adopted son?"

"Well, I wrote to Gaston about his birth mother's will, but I didn't get a response at first. That's why I asked for Christine's help."

I jumped in. "You said 'at first.' Has Gaston called you?"

"That's why I'm phoning. I just finished talking to his father, Jean-Paul. He said Gaston was on the line too, but Jean-Paul did all the talking. He wanted to know how Gaston could access the money. I told him the best thing was for Gaston to come to Philadelphia with proof of identity, and we could sort it all out in my office, but the father refused. He said Gaston was too young to travel alone, and he couldn't spare the time away to come with him. I didn't think that made sense: Gaston's nearly eighteen, after all. I could meet him at the airport—"

"How did Lemesur react?" Henderson asked.

"He seemed angry. I kept trying to talk to Gaston, ask him how he felt, how was school, things like that, but the father interrupted every time. I'm quite worried about the boy."

"How did the conversation end?"

"I mentioned the possibility of giving a local person here in Philadelphia the power of attorney to act for Gaston. Jean-Paul said he'd look into it."

There was a pause. The room was stuffy with five people crammed in. There was a sheen of sweat on

Kleinberg's forehead. I wanted to take my jacket off but thought there'd be perspiration circles under my arms. The only person keeping his cool was Henderson. He was deep in thought, staring at the ceiling.

"How about this," he said, voice thoughtful. "You suggest meeting them in Washington State, just south of the border. Surely he could get away from home for a couple of hours."

"You mean, I'd come there?"

"Not necessarily. Once Lemesur arrived here we could detain him for questioning in connection with the death of Victoria Hartman. You wouldn't have to be present—just set up the meeting."

"But what about Gaston? There's nothing to say he's involved with his father's criminal activities. I have a responsibility to him!" James sounded almost tearful. I sympathized with him. Henderson's single-minded focus on catching his man ignored any collateral damage. Maybe in my cynical past, I'd have taken the same approach. Not now. I decided to plunge in.

"I think you're right to be worried about Gaston, James. His father may be keeping him locked up. I spoke to a neighbor of his yesterday, and he said he hasn't seen Gaston for months, and he hasn't been going to school."

Every head in the room turned to me. I kept my eyes on the phone on the desk, hoping that revealing I'd staked out Lemesur's address wouldn't lead to the exposure of my humiliation—being bushwacked by the subject of my surveillance was not a good look for a police detective.

Anderson and Henderson continued discussing the logistics of getting both Lemesurs over the border while keeping Gaston out of harm's way. Once Anderson terminated the call, the meeting wound up. I was filing out of the office close behind John, when Kleinberg, speaking as if to an ill-behaved dog, said, "McQuarry! Stay!" He waited until the others except for John had left. The M.E. stood close behind me just inside the doorway; he literally had my back.

Once persuaded that John wasn't leaving, Kleinberg jabbed a finger at me. "You are out of line. You got lucky this time, ID-ing a drug kingpin, but after this case is closed you are going to be facing serious charges of officer misconduct."

After this case is closed: did that mean I'd been temporarily reinstated? I knew better than to press my luck. "Yes, sir!" I answered crisply. I thought John was getting ready to object. It wouldn't help, so I spun around and forced him out of the office ahead of me.

Chapter 36

As we exited the building, I spotted Chief Superintendent Kenneth Henderson across the street. He was looking at his phone, but I guessed he was waiting to speak to me.

"I'd love to stop for coffee, but I have to get back to the office," John said. I was glad he hadn't seen Henderson. While I appreciated John's urge to protect me, I didn't want him interfering in what could be a crucial police operation.

"Yeah, I know, dead bodies piling up," I replied cheerfully. "Hey, thanks for looking out for me in there. Let's get together soon." I strode away until John was around the corner, then doubled back across the street toward the Canadian cop.

He didn't bother with a greeting. "What's this about medical leave? Are you sick?"

"No, it's just a misunderstanding." That excuse might have diverted James Anderson, but not Henderson. He fixed me with a questioning stare.

"Who does Captain Kleinberg report to?"

"The Chief of Police, Desmond Ingram."

"What's he like?"

I shrugged, uncertain where this was going. "He's fairly new. I haven't had much contact with him. He lets Kleinberg run the detective squad—at least so far."

"Hmm. I want you and Anderson to front this

operation. I'll square it with Chief Ingram. When the Lemesurs get to the meeting, you and Anderson get the son away. A team will then move in and arrest Jean-Paul." He paused. "You do have enough to hold Jean-Paul for Hartman's murder, don't you?"

Tempting as it was to lie and say yes, Henderson deserved honesty. "We have motive—Jean-Paul definitely didn't want Victoria in Gaston's life. And we have opportunity—he was at the hotel when Victoria disappeared. But we have no forensics and no witnesses. It all depends on what Gaston knows and whether he'll testify against the only father he's ever known."

"No forensics? What about that Medical Examiner friend of yours? Could he not run some more tests on the samples collected at the post-mortem?"

"The autopsy? I'll ask him."

"Good. In the meantime, keep me informed. You have my number. And in case you can't reach me, here's the number for the senior FBI agent on the task force." My phone pinged as he messaged me the contact. I tried to look cool with it, but the idea of having the FBI as a backup resource thrilled me.

We shook hands and parted. I had to restrain myself from skipping back to my car.

****

I stopped at my apartment long enough to make and eat a sandwich and draw up a list of local law firms that might serve as a venue for James Anderson to discuss Victoria's estate with the Lemesurs. I scoped out a few of these firms from the curb before settling on Haringay & White. The four-person firm was located in a lovely old house that had been swallowed up by the commercial expansion of downtown. Opposite was a shopping center with extensive parking from which surveillance would be easy. Medical offices occupied the neighboring building, and a quiet street offered additional parking and stake-out opportunities on the other side.

Glad of my business attire, I approached the receptionist. "I'm sorry, I don't have an appointment, but I wondered if I could have a word with one of the partners?"

The receptionist smiled and invited me to sit, while she whispered into her headset. "Karen White will be with you in five minutes," she called out in a louder voice.

While I waited, I considered how to play it. I didn't have my police badge with me—that was still nestled with my gun in Kleinberg's desk. I'd stick to giving the minimum information and let someone above my pay grade fill Ms. White in on the underlying purpose of the operation later.

Karen White was a fit-looking fifty-year-old with silver hair and an outfit almost identical to mine. She didn't comment on our matching clothes but guided me into a conference room at the back of the building. There were windows on two sides. At the back, the view was of a paved space—employee parking, I surmised—that opened onto an alley. The side windows looked out at the blank wall of the medical office building—a perfect set-up for our purposes.

"I'm assisting a Philadelphia attorney, James Anderson. He's the executor of the estate of a woman called Victoria Hartman." I realized this was word-for-word what I had told Lemesur the day before when I'd had a gun in my ribs. "The beneficiary under the will lives in the Vancouver, BC area. To avoid dragging him all the way across the country, Mr. Anderson wanted to meet with him here in town—together with his father, as he's a minor—in order to verify identity and make further arrangements for the settlement of the estate."

"We're happy to help out-of-state attorneys in this way. Maybe Mr. Anderson can do the same for us one day. Any idea when this conference will take place?"

"Not yet, but we hope very soon. I'll call with details as soon as I know them."

Karen gave me her card. Another big smile from the receptionist, and I was on my way. That was easy.

I had stopped to pick up some groceries when my phone buzzed. The screen told me it was Ed, Britney's uncle.

"It's him! I just saw him outside school! He must have followed me!" The voice was not Ed's but a hysterical Britney.

"Who did you see, Britney?"

"The guy from Portland—the one who left me locked in that shitty house in Seattle—Dev called him Chef. He's here!"

"Take a breath, Britney. Where are you now?"

"I'm in Uncle Ed's car. He picked me up from school. I had to wait to call because I'm not allowed to have my own phone." The hysteria subsided as the aggrieved teenager re-emerged.

"Did Chef see you?"

"Uh, don't think so. He was talking to some kids. I recognized his wheels, too—fancy black car with tinted windows, the one he drove to Seattle with me and Dev."

"Okay, put Uncle Ed on."

Once I was satisfied that they were driving straight home and were not being followed, I disconnected and tried to reach the school liaison officer I'd tipped off earlier about the "white guys in nice cars" peddling drugs outside the high schools in the area. The call went to voicemail. I left a detailed message, but I knew that Chef would have moved on long before action would be taken on my information.

Then I remembered the new contact listed on my phone as FBI Agent Pettigrew. Did this qualify as an emergency? Should I call Henderson first? He'd be back over the border by now. Oh, hell, I couldn't be in more trouble with the higher-ups than I already was. I clicked on the agent's number.

After two rings, a female voice answered, "Field office."

"May I speak to Agent Pettigrew?"

"This is Emily Pettigrew. How can I help you?"

Blushing at my sexist assumptions, I introduced myself and explained how I had her number. "A couple of different lines of inquiry have collided. It's rather complicated."

"I'm listening." I wanted to believe her. After years of disrespect from my colleagues and being forced to go it alone, I hoped that here was an ally.

I started with my re-examination of the fentanyl OD files, and how that had led me to Frank Gutierrez, whose mother had died after she confronted the drug dealers pressuring her son. I explained that another interview had produced a tip about "white guys in nice cars" selling drugs outside high schools. Agent Pettigrew interrupted with a couple of questions, but mainly just let me talk.

"This is where it gets complicated. A few days ago, the niece of a friend turned up here. She'd been driven from Portland to Seattle and locked up in a house with three Asian women, possible victims of trafficking. Today, outside her high school, Britney saw the man who took her. She recognized his car too. She only knows him as Chef."

I heard an intake of breath. "Chef? Like the French for boss?"

"Uh, yeah. I was thinking 'cook,' but 'boss' makes more sense. Any idea who he is?"

"Yes. Larry Cremond, a Canadian living in Portland, a suspect in the fentanyl smuggling ring."

The name was familiar. "Wait a minute. I think Larry Cremond was identified as a guest at the same hotel where Marta Gutierrez was found dead in the parking lot." And the same hotel where Victoria Hartman was staying hours before her body was found. I hadn't mentioned Jean-Paul Lemesur until now; Victoria's murder had seemed unconnected with the drug smuggling operation, even if Lemesur was suspected of being a drug kingpin. "I think we need to get Chief Superintendent Henderson on this call."

A half-hour later my ear was aching from the pressure of the phone, and my groceries were wilting in the passenger seat. I'd filled in as many details as I could remember: the name of my contact in the Seattle P.D. who I'd told about the sex-trafficking victims, as well as the school liaison officer to whom I'd reported Chef's activity today. Pettigrew had patched in Henderson, who'd explained our objective to hold Lemesur on suspicion of Victoria's murder. We speculated whether Cremond had assisted Lemesur. After all, it would be hard for one man to subdue Victoria at the same time as controlling a protesting Gaston. We kicked around the possibility that Cremond had killed Marta to stop her blowing the whistle on the high school recruiters. We identified statements that needed to be taken and additional forensics tests to be completed. By the time the call ended, the FBI was committed to two simultaneous operations: providing a team to sweep in and arrest the after-school drug dealers, including, hopefully, Larry Cremond, and a swat team to effect the arrest of Jean-Paul Lemesur as soon as James Anderson and I had taken Gaston to a place of safety. I was dizzy with the speed at which weeks of my plodding solitary investigation had gelled into action.

"Good work on this," Emily Pettigrew wrapped up her summary.

"Indeed," agreed Kenneth Henderson.

I mumbled something about the role of luck and coincidence, but my whole body glowed with the praise.

Chapter 37

Sitting across from James Anderson in Haringay & White's conference room, I was strung out tight as piano wire. The last several days of inactivity waiting for this moment had been a torment. I am not a patient person at the best of times. An independent investigator, working alone and answerable to no one, I'd developed the leads and set the train in motion, but then I'd been sidelined while the official teams that comprised the drug task force took over the operational planning: no role for me. I'd cleaned my apartment until it shone, I'd run through dark streets to the point of exhaustion, and I'd spent hours pacing my living room in one-way conversation with my Cycladic statue. Her stony expression seemed to mutate from impassive to reproachful to accusing. What right had I to be frustrated when she'd been condemned to immobility for more than four thousand years? But I could only wonder how I'd got through the intervening days without a drink.

James and I had arrived half an hour early for the meeting with the Lemesurs and were greeted in the lobby by a grim-faced Karen White. The FBI had informed her of the real purpose for which we were taking over her conference room, and she was not pleased.

"I've asked everyone to work from home this afternoon. I shall be upstairs in my office, but I trust you won't need me." She turned and marched up the stairs, her stiff back communicating disapproval.

We sat in silence, waiting. When the text came through—*he's here*—I jumped. After showing the screen to James, we hurried out to the reception area. I had just read the follow-up text—*only JP*—when the front door opened and Lemesur entered. He was wearing a dark suit and a white shirt open at the neck. He had shaved off the stubble that covered his chin when we last met. Then, his hair had been covered by a baseball cap; now I saw it was cut close to the head, dark and sleek as an otter's pelt.

He smiled at both of us, his glance resting on me for a couple of seconds in recognition. "Good afternoon."

"Mr. Lemesur, I thought it was clear that Gaston needed to be here." James' voice was taut with anger.

Jean-Paul gave an apologetic shrug. "Yeah, I'm sorry, he couldn't come. A test at school, very important—he couldn't miss it." James started to speak again, but Jean-Paul overrode him. "It's okay, I have all the documents." That smile again, all teeth, no warmth. The accent had been cleaned up, but he still gave off a gangster vibe.

"No, that's not how it's done. Gaston has to be here!" I could feel James almost vibrating next to me. The placid old lawyer had turned into a warrior. I remained quiet and watchful. I wondered if the arrest team had placed mics in the building. I hoped so, but they hadn't shared the details of the operation with me.

"But when we spoke that first time, didn't you say he could appoint someone to act for him?" Lemesur spread his hands out. "Well, he's appointed me."

I remembered that when Lemesur objected to having his son travel to Philadelphia, James had suggested that

Gaston could retain a local lawyer there to represent him.

James narrowed his eyes. "Do you have a Power of Attorney signed by Gaston?"

Lemesur slid his hand into the breast of his suit jacket.

"Gun!" I screamed, and pushed James as hard as I could through the open door to the conference room. I dove in after him. I had acted on pure instinct, not having seen what Lemesur drew out of his coat, but the sound of a bullet fired at close range vindicated my reaction. James ricocheted off the conference table, colliding with me. We ended up in an undignified heap on the floor as the lobby filled with shouts of "Police!" "Get down!" "Drop the weapon!" and the reverberation of many boots. Jean-Paul must have complied, because no more shots were fired. James and I picked ourselves up but stayed out of the way until the noise receded and a door slammed.

"Are you okay?" Emily Pettigrew poked her head around the conference room door, gun drawn but pointed down at the floor. We nodded and she holstered her weapon. "He's been arrested and read his rights. We won't have any problem holding him without bail, after that stunt." Her satisfied grin changed to a frown. "What's that?" She pointed to my arm. I looked down to where the navy blue of the sleeve fabric showed a deep wine-colored stain with a black char mark at its center. Blood was seeping down my arm, running over my hand, and dripping onto the beautiful—probably valuable—Persian rug. Ms. White would have additional reasons to feel aggrieved. "You've been shot."

Damn! My only decent jacket! I hadn't felt a thing until that moment. I looked back at Agent Pettigrew, her outline now swallowed up by black mist, and disgraced myself by fainting.

****

When I came to, a paramedic had completed the blazer's destruction by cutting the sleeve open from wrist to shoulder. He applied a pressure dressing over the wound, telling me to lie still for a moment until they fetched a stretcher.

"I can walk. I've got to—"

"You've got to go to the hospital. That wound needs proper examination, cleaning and stitching," the paramedic interrupted. "You can walk to the ambulance if you like, but you'll lie on the stretcher while we take you to the ER, for your own safety."

My protests carried no weight. All I could do was tell James to take my car keys and to pick me up from the hospital as soon as possible. When we arrived at the Emergency Room, I was whizzed past the other poor saps waiting, delivery by ambulance and a gunshot wound trumping less dramatic but possibly more painful injuries. The wound was cleaned, X-rayed, sutured and re-bandaged, and I was given the good news that the bullet was small caliber, had missed the brachial artery and the bone, although there would be scarring. Then my other arm was hooked up to a bag of IV fluids and I was shunted into a curtained-off cubicle to wait. And wait.

The IV bag was empty. My calls to the nurses and doctors who hurried past the gap in the curtains went unheeded. With no phone or wall clock to tell me the time, it felt like hours had passed. I was on the point of pulling out the IV shunt myself, when James leaned into the cubicle, holding a plastic drawstring bag containing my belongings.

"We must find Gaston," he said by way of greeting. "I'm so worried his father has hurt him."

"Agreed. Let's get out of here. Can you find someone to…" I waved at my tether. James returned with a nurse, who unhooked me, then provided a small number of painkillers and a sheet of wound-care instructions. After signing some insurance forms without reading them, I was discharged.

"I think our best course is to call Chief Superintendent Henderson," I suggested as we left the hospital building. It was fully dark now, and the cold hit me like a wall. I staggered.

"You need a warm coat, and something to eat," James had reverted from Mad Max to kindly grandfather. I keep a stash of spare clothes in my car for stake-outs and quick costume changes. James helped me thread my damaged arm through a zip-front hoodie. He insisted on driving, and for once I was grateful to be a passenger. He turned north on the highway, away from downtown. While waiting for me, he had done some searching on the internet. At the next exit, he turned into a small outlet mall with two stand-alone fast-food restaurants fronting the interstate. We opted for the burgers and fries joint over the Mexican one, and as James joined the line at the counter, I called Henderson.

"Did you hear? They've got Jean-Paul, but he didn't bring Gaston. James and I are worried."

"Yes, I heard from Agent Pettigrew that the operation was successful. *All* the operations, in fact. The sweep of high schools netted three individuals yet to be identified. No drugs, though, so we'll need those witnesses you mentioned. The Seattle PD raided the house lodging the suspected sex-trafficking victims and found three Asian women. One was pretty far gone and had to be revived with Narcan. The other two are talking, but they haven't found an interpreter yet." Henderson sounded pleased with himself, even though the RCMP hadn't been involved.

"But what about Gaston? We're on our way to Vancouver to try and find him."

"I wouldn't rush up here. As soon as I heard from Pettigrew, we executed a search warrant at the Lemesur address. Gaston's not on the premises, although there are signs he's been living there recently, maybe held captive." His calm was irritating. "No drugs in the house, but we've taken computers and phones, so we hope to get something off them. And we've put out what I think you folks call an APB for the boy. We'll find him."

When I relayed this information to James, neither of us shared Henderson's bland confidence. As we dug into our food, we speculated about what might have happened to Gaston. On one point we did agree with the Canadian: we'd serve no useful purpose crossing the border that evening. It was already close to eight o'clock.

My arm was throbbing. I downed a couple of the painkillers with my diet soda and was about to suggest I drop James back at his hotel when I noticed a knot of people in the parking lot. They were gathered around an older model American sedan.

"Hey, that's my car!" A man seated a couple of tables away rushed past us and out the exit. We watched him approach the crowd of people. Conversation ensued, which we couldn't hear but involved much gesticulating. After a few minutes, the car's owner waved the others away and pulled out his keys. He inserted the keys in the trunk and slowly lifted the lid. The bystanders crowded around again, impeding our view. The owner, assisted by another man, seemed to be extracting something from the trunk. As the men stood upright again, the onlookers parted to reveal a smaller figure dressed in sweatshirt, jeans and sneakers.

Mirroring James' open mouth and wide eyes, I asked in a whisper, "Could that be…Gaston?" That would be a coincidence beyond belief. Intrigued, we left our half-eaten food to go outside and see what was going on.

"You need to take him back and turn him in to Border Patrol," opined an officious woman with big hair.

"I haven't got time to go back—I'm due in Seattle." The car owner was irritated. "He's nothing to do with me."

"But you brought him across the border," reasoned another onlooker.

"You should at least call the police. They can take him back," the big-haired woman suggested. Through all this, the subject under discussion looked warily from face to face, saying nothing.

"You call the police, then!" The car owner had had enough. He opened the driver's side door, climbed in, and started his engine. I steered the boy aside, to prevent him being run over as the car reversed and drove off.

The crowd began to melt away except for the big-haired woman who pulled out her phone in a self-important manner. "*Someone* needs to report this!"

I decided to intervene. "I'm with the police— Coalport PD, Detective Sergeant McQuarry." I wished I had a warrant card to flash, but she seemed to believe me in spite of my disheveled appearance, and backed off. Maybe sober-suited James Anderson nodding confirmation helped. "What's your name, kid?"

The boy's chin came up and his eyes narrowed with suspicion. I had a flash of myself at the same age: defiant and solitary.

"You look hungry. How about we buy you a burger?"

The boy shrugged and followed us back inside. This time, I went to the counter to order, while James shepherded the young illegal immigrant to our table. By the time I returned with a jumbo burger, large fries and a soft drink, James had his arm around the boy's heaving shoulders as his face streaked with tears and snot.

The lawyer looked up and I slid the tray across in front of them. "I told him Victoria Hartman was dead."

Chapter 38

John spent the first week of the year catching up on the holiday backlog of bodies and trying to find gaps in the autopsy reports he had written during the early months of his tenure as Medical Examiner. He'd come into the job confident in his academic forensic skills, but, when it came to crime, Christine had taught him that objective scientific inquiry had to be tempered with life experience, intuition, and sometimes even guesswork. He'd been wrong about Victoria Hartman; how many other errors and omissions had he made?

In his limited free time, John attacked the redecoration of his dilapidated farmhouse. Stripping layers of wallpaper and sanding window frames left space for his thoughts to go over the same old ground of his relationship with Christine—if indeed they had a relationship. They were alike: both independent types reluctant to accept help or advice and impatient with those not as smart as they were. That should make them compatible. But Christine's obsessions and her inability to check her impulses or curb her tongue made him wary of her. What rankled him most was her failure to acknowledge the personal changes he'd made, his efforts to be a better person. He knew he'd been wrong to go to Kleinberg with his concerns about Christine's mental state, but he'd wanted to put that right—and she hadn't let him. She didn't seem to recognize what it cost him to admit his professional shortcomings. In fact, he doubted whether Christine spent much time thinking about his feelings at all. Perhaps he should concede they would never be more than friends.

At nine-thirty, John decided he'd done enough work for the night and went into the kitchen to reward himself with a whiskey before tackling the task of cleaning up. His mind was still on Christine, so when he picked up his phone he was unsurprised to see a text from her: *U home? Be there in ten with guests.*

Typical! No details, no "may I" or "please." Just a bald announcement. Nevertheless, he felt a buzz of excitement as he put down his now-empty glass and hurried back into the living room to fold dropcloths and steep paintbrushes in mineral spirit.

He had assumed one guest would be James Anderson, the Philadelphia lawyer in town to meet with Victoria's son. Christine had been cagey about the specifics, but he knew the rendezvous was important. When Christine arrived, she ushered in an older man who fit the lawyer's profile, as well as a teenage boy.

John stepped forward to shake hands. Christine dispensed with formal introductions and got straight to the point. "Gaston needs a safe place to stay for a few days."

"What? Here?" John stuttered. He waved a hand at the paint cans and other decorating paraphernalia stacked against the wall. "I haven't even started on the bedrooms yet—"

"For Christ's sake, John, it's not an *Architectural Digest* photo shoot! The boy needs a place to stay while we sort out his status."

Anderson intervened with a calming hand gesture.

"Gaston came into the country in a rather…unorthodox manner, but he's an important witness in a criminal case."

Christine's irritation was not to be appeased. "Look, you foisted Britney on me without notice. What's your problem?"

For the first time since she arrived, John took in Christine's pallor and the dark circles under her eyes. She was holding herself in a strange manner, her arm stiffly angled across her body. "What's wrong?"

She shrugged, then winced with the movement. "I got shot. Jean-Paul Lemesur was arrested today."

"Let me take a look—I'm a doctor," John moved forward, but Christine raised her hand palm out to stop him.

"I've been to the hospital. It's all taken care of." She slumped, suddenly exhausted. "I need a drink." Seeing John's frown, she added, "Just a glass of water for me. Tea, coffee, anyone?"

John took drink orders—tea for Anderson, water for Gaston. Christine followed him into the kitchen. While he filled the kettle, she leaned back against the countertop. "Sorry for snapping at you. It's been a long day."

John passed her a glass of water. "Okay, I can see you've been through the wringer. Of course I'll help. The spare bedroom's a bit dusty, but it's warm and dry. Tell me what's going on."

Christine took a sip of water. "They're holding Jean-Paul on the shooting charge while we line up the evidence for charging him with Victoria's murder. Gaston's statement is key. But Jean-Paul will have made his one phone call by now—he has criminal connections on both sides of the border, and he's ruthless. His goons will be looking for Gaston. We could send Gaston back with James to his hotel in town, but we have to assume Lemesur's friends know James' connection to the case—he wouldn't be safe."

After John and Christine joined the others in the living room, conversation stumbled along. Everyone was tired. Even James' well-mannered efforts to put Gaston at ease slowed to a stop.

"Are you okay to drive?" John asked Christine when her eyelids drooped shut for the third time.

She nodded at James Anderson. "He's my chauffeur."

Soon after, leaving Gaston dozing on the sofa, John followed James and Christine to the front door. James went outside to start the car. Christine turned back to John. "Thanks for doing this. I'll check in with you tomorrow."

He wanted to wrap his arms around her and hold her close—comfort her—but realized it might hurt her arm. Anyway, she would reject any protective gesture. Instead, he bent forward and kissed her cheek. For a moment she leaned against him and he breathed in the scent of her hair.

"Goodnight." No, he didn't want them just to be friends.

Chapter 39

I slept for eleven hours straight—the longest in ages. Perhaps that second dose of painkillers helped. I woke feeling pretty good, considering. There was still work to be done, but Jean-Paul was in jail and Gaston was safe—for now.

I placed a call to Chief Superintendent Henderson, knowing I should have contacted him last night but I was too wiped out. The call went to voicemail. "We have located Gaston Lemesur in the United States and are taking steps to secure a statement in the Victoria Hartman case." I used this formal, oblique language fearing Henderson might react poorly to Gaston's illegal entry into the country. He might want to extradite him back to Canada, which would put him even more at risk.

I shouldn't have worried. Henderson called me back almost immediately, eager to talk about the search of Lemesur's townhouse, not asking about Gaston's whereabouts. "We're getting some good stuff off Lemesur's laptop and the phones we found—names or codenames for the mid-level dealers. With luck and some hard work from the cybertechs, we should be able to disrupt his whole fentanyl smuggling organization."

"That's great," I responded. "I'll just continue coordinating with the FBI and local law enforcement on the Hartman case then, shall I?"

"Yes. Keep me posted on Lemesur." He rang off.

My next call was to Agent Pettigrew. She was much more engaged. "How's your arm? What did the ER doctors say?"

I gave her a quick summary, then changed the subject. "We found Gaston Lemesur. He's convinced his father killed Victoria, but he didn't actually see anything. In fact, he was hoping she was still alive, just scared off by his dad. So we might need more to convict Jean-Paul for murder."

"Hmm. Remember we speculated that JP might have needed help to overpower Victoria and get her out of the hotel without anyone noticing? Well, we managed to round up three likely suspects yesterday—stateside members of his fentanyl operation. One of them is Larry Cremond—"Chef"—the guy who kidnapped your little friend and dumped her in a sex-trafficking den in Seattle. Now that we've found a Cambodian interpreter, we've got a solid case against Cremond for drug- *and* sex-trafficking. I bet he'd trade what he knows about JP to escape a murder charge on top of that."

"*If* he knows anything. But you're right, Lemesur did have help. Gaston told us that after his dad dragged him out of the hotel lobby, he was shoved into the back of a car driven by another man. They took him out into the county and locked him in some derelict outbuildings. He has no idea where he was or how long he was left, but when they came back for him it was completely dark. Same driver took them to rendezvous with another car, and Jean-Paul and Gaston crossed back into Canada at some isolated little border post sometime before dawn."

"If the driver was Cremond, we're in business!" Pettigrew was excited. "Let's get Gaston to the FBI holding facility for an ID."

"Um, slight hiccup. Technically, Gaston's in the U.S. illegally. His dad took his passport away, so he smuggled himself in." I hoped my faith in Emily Pettigrew wasn't misplaced. If she turned out to be a rigid rule follower, she'd hand Gaston over to the Canadians and it would take several miles of red tape to get him south of the border again for the identification.

"No problem. Gaston's passport was with JP's personal effects handed over when he was processed. I can sort it out with the Customs and Border Patrol and there'll be no questions asked. How soon can you get him here? Oh, and we'll need Britney whatever-her-name-is, too, for a formal identification of Cremond as the man who kidnapped her."

"Sure, I'll arrange that." Then I had another idea. "I think I told you about Marta Gutierrez, the woman who confronted the drug dealers recruiting at her son's high school and ended up dead? I wonder if her son Frank might recognize Cremond too? It's a long shot, but it wouldn't hurt to have the threat of another murder inquiry hanging over him."

"Good thinking," Emily agreed. "The more pressure, the faster Cremond'll cave. I want to nail Lemesur for murder before the Canadians develop their drugs case and try to extradite him for trial." Canada and the U.S. might be "children of a common mother" but international cooperation was not high on Emily's list of law enforcement priorities. I wondered what it would take to get a transfer into her FBI unit.

We talked through details of time and place for a few minutes, then disconnected. Almost immediately, my phone chirped again.

"Whassup, McQuarry?" Myers sounded cheerful.

"Calling to invite you to drinks tomorrow night to celebrate my promotion to sergeant."

"Yeah, thanks but no thanks."

"Aw, come on! The squad wants to see you—you're our hero!"

"Mmm, sorry. I have plans."

"What plans?"

"I'll think of something."

"Don't be like that. Kleinberg won't be there. He's in Florida."

"Huh?"

"Yeah, using up his accumulated leave time before he retires."

"Kleinberg's retiring?" I squeaked. That was worth celebrating.

"Well, he's twenty-five years on the job, his kid just graduated college, and his wife wants to live somewhere warm. Word is, he's interviewing for a private security job down there." Myers was taking pleasure in being the one to break the news.

"Wait! Kleinberg's *married*? And has *kids*?"

"*A* kid. He's always talking about his darling daughter—straight A's and star of the soccer team."

Well, he never talked to me about her. Or perhaps I never listened. I felt out of touch and even a bit nostalgic for the fug of the squad room—burnt coffee and male sweat. "Maybe I'll think about it. Usual place?"

Myers let out a chortle of victory. "Great! First round's on me."

A smile crept over my face—was I really looking forward to watching a bunch of overweight white boys get drunk? Weird.

Chapter 40

The noise level had driven most of the non-law enforcement drinkers out of the bar. I was thinking of making my getaway too when I felt a tap on my shoulder. I turned to face the Chief of Police.

"Can I get you a drink? Gin and tonic?" he said, indicating the glass in my hand.

"It's just soda water, but no, thanks, I'm fine." Surprised to see the Chief at this kind of party, I stood up straighter and fought the urge to salute.

"How's the arm?"

"Healing nicely, sir. Stitches come out tomorrow."

"Fit for duty after that?"

"Definitely." Could it be that easy to get back into the department?

"You'll have to pass a psychological evaluation first." Not so easy then. "I'll set it up. We need you back soonest. You've heard Kleinberg's out?" I nodded, intrigued by the Chief's wording: "out," not "retiring." "So, Sergeant McQuarry, you're the ranking officer in charge." He must have seen my look of horror because he continued, "Don't worry, I know you're not suited for a desk job. I'm already interviewing possible replacements."

Myers had spotted the senior officer's arrival and was steaming across the room preparing to kiss ass. The Chief turned to say in a quiet voice, "Good job, by the way. Fine detective work—even if you were on leave." He grinned at me, then stepped forward to congratulate the new sergeant.

****

Due to budget cuts, the department no longer had an in-house psychologist to perform fitness-for-duty evaluations. Instead, the work was contracted out to a roster of local professionals. I was scheduled to meet with a Dr. Evelyn Fielding at an address which turned out to be both her office and home: a townhouse perched on the hillside overlooking the bay.

I rang the front doorbell and was greeted by a volley of dog barks. The door opened six inches to reveal the face and a body slice of a fiftyish woman with long gray hair, dressed in jeans and sweater. I introduced myself and said why I was there.

"Do you mind if we do this outside? It's a lovely day and this monster needs a walk. Just a minute." Without waiting for my agreement, she shut the door. She opened it a minute later, now dressed in a puffy jacket and with the dog—a highland terrier—on a leash. She patted her pockets, muttering, "Keys, poop bags, treats," before giving me her full attention.

"There's a park up this way with great views. Shall we?" She pointed up the street and we set off. She chatted about the weather, the dog—"he's fine once he gets to know you,"—and commented on the housing market. I contributed a few responsive grunts.

After about five minutes, she turned to face me and said, "What is it you said you needed me to do?"

Was this a trick question? A strategy to confuse me before she grilled me? I replied hesitantly, "Sign off on my psychological readiness to go back to work with the police department."

"Right. You were placed on leave because…?"

"My boss saw signs of stress." I could have gone on a rant about how unfair it all was, how John had set me up, and how Kleinberg had jumped on the chance to get rid of me, but I knew that would make me sound paranoid. Plus—and I'd had plenty of time to think this through—being placed on leave had been a wake-up call, perhaps the best thing that could have happened to me.

"Yes. Of course. No problem." Dr. Fielding was a little out of breath after the climb. "Lovely view, isn't it? Let's sit." She indicated a bench looking out over the roofs below, the coastal road and the water. A fitful sun painted silver bands across the bay. Seabirds swooped and screamed.

I felt an obligation to break the silence. "Do you do a lot of these fitness-for-duty evaluations?"

"No, you're my first." She laughed. I wondered if she had even read my file. She continued, "Actually, I work with trauma patients—survivors of mass shootings, serial rape, childhood sexual abuse, incest—that kind of thing."

I gasped. "That must be so hard. Can you help them?"

She answered slowly, "Yes, counseling helps through the immediate shock. But trauma's a gift that keeps on giving. You never really get over it, but there are ways to manage it. I try to help patients choose the healthy ways."

We sat together looking out at the horizon where the silvery sea met the flat gray sky. The dog had fallen asleep across Dr. Fielding's feet. I relaxed, relishing the fresh air and the undemanding company. I might even have closed my eyes for a minute.

"Losing your parents when you were sixteen was traumatic, I think."

So she *had* read my file. I sat up sharply and let out a bark of laughter. "I wasn't traumatized by their deaths—I was liberated!" Christ, I'd blown it now: she'd think I was a psychopath.

"They abused you." It was a statement, not a question.

"Yes." I breathed out the word, the first time I had acknowledged the truth to another person.

"Makes it hard to trust anyone, doesn't it?"

I nodded, still facing the horizon.

"And not trusting means you can't commit to relationships."

I nodded again. After a while, I began to talk. I told her about seeing Victoria on that mortuary table: my dopplegänger. Obsessed with identifying her and finding out about her background, I'd become convinced she was murdered. I described my inquiries carried out under cover of the joint drug task force and the murder wall I'd constructed in my spare bedroom. I spoke about my drinking, the nightmares and suicidal thoughts, the humiliating incident that led to me being transported home in a police patrol car.

"So the only relationship I've been able to commit to is with a dead woman."

Dr. Fielding sat with all this for a while. At least, I thought she was considering it. For all I knew she was making a grocery shopping list. The winter sun sank towards the water. The dog roused and shook himself.

"Time for your dinner, young man," Dr. Fielding said. We started down the hill.

As we approached the psychologist's home, I couldn't resist asking, "Will you pass me as fit for duty?"

She looked at me in surprise. "Of course! Didn't I say so earlier? 'No problem!'" She took in my relieved expression. "I'll send my report this afternoon. The Chief wants you at your desk first thing tomorrow. I'm told you're a fine detective, and I can quite believe it."

"So what was all this...this...?" I was at a loss for words. I'd just bared my innermost soul, my darkest moments.

"They pay me for an hour. You might as well get their money's worth."

After a moment, I started laughing and she joined in. As we shook hands, she added, "If you ever need to talk, just give me a call. I have a special rate for the police."

I told her I would, just to be polite.

Epilog: Six Months Later

I was over at John's place when Gaston's email arrived in his inbox. I've been spending quite a bit of time at John's house, helping with the redecorating, and, after the seasons changed, working in the overgrown yard. To my surprise, I enjoy the outdoor labor—I've never had a garden and haven't been much of a nature lover. I'm not giving up my apartment though. After a day with John, I feel the need to retreat there for time on my own. On my own, except for my Victoria: her stone inscrutability is still my anchor.

After he scanned Gaston's email, John read it aloud to me. Gaston finished high school in Philadelphia, living with James Anderson's adult daughter, who has a teenager of her own at home. Hard work and determination allowed him to graduate on time, despite missing a couple of months of school in the fall. He's eighteen now, and independently wealthy, thanks to Victoria Hartman's legacy. In the email, he admitted he felt unprepared for adult life, college, or living alone. Since his adopted mother's death six years ago, his father had become more and more controlling, monitoring his friendships, not even allowing him to learn to drive. In Philadelphia he struggled to adjust to new freedoms and opportunities, wise enough to rely on James for guidance. He recognized he needs to take some steps towards independence, which brought him to the point of the email.

"Although James and his family have been very kind, I don't feel at home in Philadelphia. I miss the Pacific Northwest but have no real ties to the Vancouver area. James obtained my original birth certificate showing my U.S. parentage, so I have U.S. citizenship. I want to live in Coalport. Can I stay with you until I find my feet? I could take some classes at the community college and get a part-time job. I have to be in Coalport for the trial in November anyway." The date of Jean-Paul's trial for Victoria's murder is set for a mere year and a month after the crime. Larry Cremond is cooperating with the prosecution. In exchange for pleading guilty to kidnapping, sex- and drug-trafficking, with a minimum sentence of fifteen years in prison, he will avoid being charged with murder.

Before sanity returned, I felt a momentary pang of jealousy that Gaston wasn't asking to move in with *me*. But Gaston formed a bond with John over the days he spent in hiding with him, and although I've made some advances in self-restraint since the dark days of last winter, John is still the adult in the room. After thinking about it for a while, I also understood how weird it would be for Gaston to live with his birth mother's near-identical twin.

"He's going to need a lot of support," John said. "Those years in Vancouver with his father must have been traumatic."

"And I know just the therapist who can help," I offered. I've been back to Dr. Fielding several times— just for a chat, I'm not a client. If she bills the Police Department, it's none of my business. We walk the dog up the hill and sit on the same bench overlooking the bay.

We talk about work, mostly. The squad room's different without Kleinberg—still the same disgusting smell but the atmosphere is clearer somehow—more cheerful. I've come to realize that I wasn't the only victim of Kleinberg's bullying. His replacement helps the mood: a fifty-year-old Black woman who moved from leading a larger detective squad in a Boston suburb to our small department in order to be close to aging parents. She's fair and methodical, no drama, and she doesn't try to micromanage me. We get on fine. It was fun to watch the guys walk around her on eggshells—scared any offhand remark would be taken as racist or sexist—but they're getting used to her now. And the enforced sensitivity training did them no harm.

Frank Gutierrez will not obtain the satisfaction of seeing his mother's murderer brought to justice. He identified Cremond as one of the men Marta had confronted, but further testing of samples taken at her autopsy didn't provide a DNA link with Cremond. However, the revised autopsy report did include a finding of possible foul play, removing the prior conclusion suggesting that his mother's death was a self-administered drug overdose. At least her name has been cleared.

I keep in touch with Frank and his sister, slipping them the occasional gift card which might make the difference between new kicks and a pair salvaged from the charity bin. With the support of his community, Frank is turning into a decent young man. He made the varsity baseball team, and his English has improved rapidly. John and I went to a couple of games to cheer him on. His sister Gloria, too shy to talk, sat next to us. Even the ever-protective Teresa acknowledged us with a nod.

"We have to keep Britney away from Gaston—she'll eat him alive." I was back to discussing the email. Ed and Perry keep Britney on a short leash, using the withdrawal of phone and driving privileges to keep her in line. She has a fatal attraction for bad boys but stays away from drugs—as far as we know. Ed is convinced I'm a good influence, roping me into expeditions to the mall or the hairdressing salon. I protest but secretly enjoy her energy and exuberance. Despite her atrocious taste in clothes and hair color, she shows some serious artistic talent.

Any hope that rounding up Jean-Paul Lemesur's network would stop the flow of fentanyl over the border was short-lived. The drug is too cheap, too easy to transport, and too powerfully addictive to stamp out. The continuing work of the joint drug task force brings me together with Kenneth Henderson and Emily Pettigrew for occasional meetings. We exchange leads and compare data, drink too much coffee, and leave depressed. My desire to transfer to the FBI has waned. At least in Coalport, there's the occasional bicycle theft—"I was just borrowing it!"—or absent-minded old lady shoplifter to vary the diet of drug-related crime.

John laughs when I say I'm putting my faith in the younger generation: Gaston, Frank, and yes, even Britney. "You sound middle-aged."

Then I have to remind him he's ten years older than me and was *born* middle-aged, which usually ends in him throwing a pillow at me.

We're friends now.

Acknowledgments

Loners is my second Pacific Northwest mystery. After writing novels set in Atlanta, France, Latvia and the U.K., it's a joy to find inspiration close to home.

Thanks to everyone at The Wild Rose Press, and especially to my editor Nan Swanson. As always, I am grateful to my writing group (Linda Lambert, Amory Peck, Betsy Gross, Lynn McInster, Frances Howard Snyder, Aaron Palmer, and Lisa Dailey) for their perceptive critiques and unflagging encouragement. I rely on this group for support and accountability.

A word about the author...

Marian Exall is an award-winning author of mysteries and historical fiction. She grew up in England and lived in France and Belgium before emigrating to the USA, raising a family and pursuing a career as a lawyer.

She now lives in the Pacific Northwest, where she enjoys hiking, gardening and cooking. And of course writing.

Find out more at https://www.marianexall.com

****

Also by this author and published by The Wild Rose Press, Inc.:

Daughters of Riga
Six Degrees of Death

www.ingramcontent.com/pod-product-compliance
Lightning Source LLC
Chambersburg PA
CBHW052024020726
47501CB00004B/1236